# DEPORTED
## *into* DESTINY

## Willie Maeobia

Deported Into Destiny



ISBN-13: 978-1-946229-81-6 (ebook)
ISBN-13: 978-1-946229-82-3 (paperback)

# Contents

# Chapter 1

# Early Childhood Upbringing on Ramos Island

I was born on a tiny Pacific island nation known as the Solomon Islands, a former colony of the British that attained independence in July 7, 1978. The country was divided into nine provincial jurisdictions. The islands are very rich in natural resources. These resources remain untapped because the resource owners do not have the knowledge, mechanisms, or technology to convert those resources into cash and thus, improve their daily livelihood. Not only do they lack the technology, but they also do not have the management skills that would enable them to extract these resources to realize the greatest benefits.

And so, foreigners come in, seize the opportunity, and reap the benefits of the local resources, leaving these local owners with very little, or even nothing. Furthermore, these foreigners do not even know how to manage the resources that they extract. They take these resources for their own personal gains and forget all about the future of these poor resource owners. The economy of the country is aid-dependent, and since attaining independence, the Solomon Islands have been bombarded with foreign aid from the international donor community. Today, my country is still leaping, struggling, and drowning in debt, trying to free itself from the grips and claws of aid dependency but to no avail.

My name is Maduku Mamata. I was raised in obscurity on Ramos Island. I was involved and engaged in subsistence agriculture with my parents at an early age. I was five feet, two or three inches tall with clear eyes, black hair, brown eyes, and an easy smile. I was an introvert, a gentleman, and nearly a saint. I went to Fa'ato Primary School to learn arithmetic and literature. My parents set up a strict schedule for me so that I could execute my responsibilities outside of school and do my homework. These responsibilities included fetching water from the spring for cooking and drinking, collecting wood for cooking and light, and feeding the pigs in the evening before sunset. My parents were tough on me when I was tender and easy to bend. I was trained to be a man very early in life. In the event my parents might not be around someday, I could still manoeuvre through life's perils and challenges in their absence. My parents must have felt the inevitable because I lost them to tuberculosis and malaria when I was eleven years old. Life has been not the same ever since.

After my parents went into the spirit world, I lived with my aunt, Ms. Rose Mary, my father's sister. My aunt was strict and tough on discipline. She was hearty and generous, but not lenient to idleness or laziness. She was a hard worker, ploughing the earth and growing food for her daily survival. I fit in perfectly under my aunt's guidance because I had been raised properly by my parents. I grew in discipline and integrity under the sole custody of my aunt.

My aunt never went to school. Her father did not have the money to send her. A girl going to school was not compulsory back in the day. Investing in a girl's education is considered unprofitable because when she marries out of the family and lives with her husband, she is giving and contributing to the community that she marries into. Every time she visits her family, it is costly for the father to send her back to her husband. It's a liability investing in a girl's education. The return on investment is missing from the equation. And so, my aunt helped her mom with the house chores and went to the garden and fed the pigs. That was her life.

She married and had two kids. One day, her husband went fishing in the ocean and never came home. A search was conducted but was eventually called off. She had to go through life as a widow, raising two kids on her own. She often questioned why life was so unfair, but she was determined to give her kids a better life. She didn't want them to go through what she had been through as a little girl, never getting an education because her parents didn't have the money to send her to school. She wanted it to be different for her children and her grandchildren. She wanted a generational change for her children and for me, her nephew. She took me and raised me as her own.

There was no favouritism. She treated all three of us equally. She sent us to school to get an education because she knew the world was changing, and we must change with it. She continued to instil in us hard work, sacrifice, and self-discipline for what we wanted to achieve in life. At breakfast, before we went to school, she unleashed on us the values and disciplines to adhere to and abide by to keep us on the right path. She constantly repeated and reminded us of the importance of hard work, self-respect and respect for others, and the sacrifice of leisure activities for something of a greater gain. She learned these values from her father. They made her into the woman that she was, and now she was transferring them to my cousins and to me.

Although she was denied having an education due to her father's financial constraints, she wanted her daughter to be a nurse because she was kind, compassionate, and caring. Working in the medical field as a nurse would be a very rewarding experience for her because of her positive attitude and nurturing personality. With us, she wanted me to be a clerk in an office, and her son to be a carpenter.

She was tough on us, reminding us to be diligent in school and in our homework. After school, we were assigned tasks to keep the family moving forward, and these tasks kept us busy and occupied, leaving less room for bad influence and even worse company. I was already familiar with these chores because they were very nearly the same as the responsibilities I had had under my parents' guidance.

We were only allowed to play soccer if we completed the tasks assigned to us for the day. If a task was unfinished or undone, then there was no playing soccer for an entire week. She told us every day to work hard at everything, both in and out of school because we were orphans and our future was entirely in our hands.

All three of us did extremely well in school. I loved to browse the dictionary when the teacher was not present. I loved finding new words and their meanings. I did very well in my spelling exams, and my classmates called me the "dictionary man." I didn't care because I always beat them in our spelling exams.

# Chapter 2

# From Asi Asi, Auki Town to the Capital City

One Saturday morning, something happened that altered the course of my life forever. It was a pivotal and defining moment. My cousin, a few other boys from Bubulu village, and I went to the beach to see a tourist boat berthing in the harbor. Having a tourist boat in the harbor for the first time in thirty years was fascinating. On our way back from the beach, we walked through a cocoa plantation. There was a pile of cocoa fertilizer packets piled beside the path. They looked pretty much the same as a packet of salt for seasoning because of the wrapping and color.

Adam Mola, one of the boys, thought they were salt and took a packet home. He hid it under his shirt from the other boys because he thought they might report him to the owner or his mother for stealing. Taking other people's property doesn't reflect well on the reputation of parents. In the public eye, it is thought to be a failure of parents to apply discipline at home. Adam could not read or write, and so he thought it was a packet of salt. He got home and poured the whole packet into a salt container without his mother's knowledge. His mother couldn't read or write either. She returned from the river and poured two spoonfuls of the white stuff into the soup she was cooking. After eating the soup, they both vomited profusely and were rushed to the hospital. They passed away a few days later due to internal complications. If Adam and his mom had been literate, this tragedy could have been avoided. Especially Adam since he was the one who took the packet of salt home that day.

The bodies of Adam and his mother were buried in a graveyard close to the hospital, but far from home. The hospital's ambulance was broken down; it had a mechanical fault in the ignition system. The part had been ordered but wasn't expected to arrive for two weeks. The family had no money to transport their bodies home for proper closure. Family members and relatives didn't have a chance to pay their respects or bid them farewell. There was a truck that could have transported them home. It was hired to carry people and goods to a wedding on the east side of the island. Torrential rain, however, made it difficult for the truck to make it to the hospital in time to transport the bodies back home. The road was waterlogged, and the possibility of getting bogged down was inevitable.

I was heartbroken and devastated when I learned that being illiterate was the major cause of their deaths. And not bringing them home because there was no availability of transport was just unacceptable. There was private transport, but Adam and his mom's family just didn't have the money to pay for the hire. They didn't have the money because they were poor. I resolved and determined from that moment to find solutions for these issues: illiteracy and lack of money. I made up my mind to rise to the challenge and pursue it with everything within me.

When I had made up my mind to find solutions to these problems at all cost, I found a passion for living. I found something bigger than my own private ambitions. I found something even greater than the threat of death engineered by humans or natural catastrophes. It was a defining moment for me. I felt obligated to address the issues of illiteracy and lack of money on my own terms. Yet, I needed a mechanism to deliver the solutions to the problems. I looked around and realized that the pig is a commercial and affordable commodity that was readily available, perhaps that was the right vehicle for delivery. I felt like I had been filled with an idea so big it occupied all my thoughts. Day and night, it was always on my mind. The thoughts never left me. I took it upon myself to make it my life's mission to bring about solutions for these two problems.

I continued attending primary education and was fortunate enough to transition to high school. After high school, I applied for a scholarship to study human resource management at St. Andrew's college in Australia. It was a prestigious award. Out of the many who applied, I was the successful applicant. I won the award. I was the first candidate in the history of the region to win a scholarship, it was a long time coming.

Before I left for college, a small event was organized by the chief. It was a tradition to send off someone who was leaving for college with a small meal, shared with family, friends, and the whole village. The chief released his blessing and well wishes on my life. In a village, everybody is family. While everybody was enjoying their food, the chief, Augustine Fanualama, stood up and uttered a few remarks of gratitude and appreciation to everybody who had shown up.

"Thank you very much, everybody, for coming. I am so honored to say that we finally have one of our very own, Mr. Maduku Mamata, who will be leaving us to study Human Resource Management at St Andrew's College overseas. I believe we are living in times where knowledge about managing our natural resources is more crucial than ever before. On my way back yesterday from town, I witnessed something appalling and sad. An expectant mother had to walk four kilometres to fetch water for drinking and cooking.

The clean water nearby her village has turned a brownish muddy color from toxic elements and substances from a logging company operating in the area, not clean and safe for cooking and drinking. I also saw a man carrying beams for his house. He walked three hours into the bush for bush materials to build a house for his family. What was that about?

Greed and personal ambition has blinded the minds of a very few individuals over communal aspirations and human life. Logging has destroyed the land and polluted the rivers. We need urgent action, bold and swift, to protect our land before we reach the point of regret. If don't act, we will end up like the village along the road.

"Having Maduku leaving to study Human Resource Management at college is our only hope and chance to make the necessary changes before we regret our cooperative failure to take action against foreign elements, coming to log our land without any knowledge about sustainable harvesting, and leaving behind ugly environmental scars on the land, causing soil infertility and erosion. I believe, there is a better way to harvest our natural resources. We have resources in abundance that we haven't touch yet. But we need the management skills to better manage what we harvest," he said.

The people agreed with what the chief had said. I also thanked the chief and the people for the unwavering support they have shown me prior to my departure for college. I asked them to remember me in their prayers. I also asked the parents to get involved in their kids' education, making sure they learn what they need to learn. I told them to check to see if their children are doing their homework. I explained it is vital to the success of a child. "A child's superior academic performance at school is a reflection of good parental support at home. Without that parental rapport and support, our kids won't achieve their highest potential in school," I said.

The morning after the function, I caught a pickup truck to the town to board a ship to the capital, so I could organize my visa and travel arrangements. I arrived at the small town and paid for my boat ticket. I was given a concession fare. The small town was packed with people from the villages, displaying what they grew in their backyards and gardens. The market was situated close to the beach, a perfect location to feel the ocean breeze and hear the waves splashing on the shoreline. The small town was the central hub that facilitated all the business transactions for the producers and consumers in and around the island. It was administered by the council. The council charged a modest fee for the maintenance and general upkeep of the facilities at the market.

I bought a packet of fish and chips at one of the lock-up shops at the market. The fish and chips were crispy and delicious, and well cooked, too. The person who cooked the fish and chips guessed my taste and preference very well, not too oily and not too much dough.

After I finished eating my fish and chips, I went to a small corner shop to buy water. When the owner saw me, I knew that he was not local, "Hello, how can I help you?" he asked. "You look like you are not from here. Are you local or from any of the areas nearby?"

"Yes, you are right. I'm not from here, sorry. Actually, I'm from Asi Asi village in the North,"

"So what are you selling at the market?" he continued.

"I'm not selling anything, I'm traveling to the capital to organize my visa and travel arrangements to study at college," I explained.

"Oh wow, that's awesome!" he said.

"I got a scholarship to study Human Resource Management at college. I am the first candidate in my village and in the entire district to win a prestigious award to study abroad," I said.

"Wow! Congratulations sir! I've heard about Asi Asi village. Some of my customers who come in here, they're from your village. They are nice people. They smile and talk to you, even if you are meeting them for the first time. I talked to some people from that village when they came in to buy groceries and other household needs and utensils. And too often, I've heard them express their frustrations and disappointments of the underdevelopment of that region. Their elected officials keep failing to deliver on promises they made during political campaigns. The people have been living and waiting in limbo to realize industrial development and growth for the region. I feel for the people. You know, the elected officials forget that they are dispensable, that they are here on this planet only for so long.

One day they will die and leave the planet. No one lives forever. That's the sad reality that everyone is facing. With the realization that we are all dispensable, we should endeavour to do everything in our power to make life a little bit better and sweeter for those we claim to represent in high office," the shop owner said. "And your constituency is the largest on the island, with huge manpower and untapped resources. Once manpower and the resources are being utilized and converted, your constituency will be the most powerful and the wealthiest on the island. I hope you will make a good leader in your field of study when you finish college, and come back to train and equip your people to be productive and industrious, so they can participate and contribute to the development of the region and the wider economy as a whole. At the moment, most people, including young people who leave school, are disillusioned and disoriented. They are not trained and equipped to maneuver and weather the storms and challenges life is throwing at them. They do not possess the necessary skills and tools to handle and manage life effectively.

"Most of these young people resort to crime and become a menace to their communities. This is the struggle and the reality that most of our communities are grappling with right now. And it demands new ways of thinking to successfully chart and navigate the challenges of youth unemployment and underdevelopment in our respective constituencies and communities, leading into the future. It is possible and achievable. We have the resources and the manpower to make it happen. We just need someone with a heart to establish a model that will eventually be duplicable and spill over into other communities and constituencies."

I listened attentively to every single word that came out of the man's mouth. What he said made perfect sense. He looked at his watch and gave me some tuna, bread, and soft drinks. He didn't charge me. It seemed he was excited and impressed to meet me, and he wished me the best of luck and said he hoped to see me one day as a prominent leader, representing and leading our people to discover their calling and mission in life. I said thank you to the man with a firm handshake and walked out of the man's shop with a heavy heart. It was a heavy burden to see my people realize, release, and maximize their potential and live their dreams before they went to their graves.

I was greatly disturbed as I walked down to the wharf. I stood on the wharf and looked back at the market and the small town, my eyes welling with the great sadness that was in my heart. The shop owner's words just kept ringing louder and louder in my head. My heart was ripped and torn, and I knew that something had to be done. The man's words were like fire in my bones. I convinced myself that I was the one because I saw the plight of my people. "What are you going to do about it?" I asked myself. It seemed as life was telling me to do something about it. I felt that I was responsible because I saw and understood the problems of my people. What a burden to bear. What a burden to carry.

The captain announced that passengers traveling to the capital could start boarding, and visitors not intending to travel needed to disembark the vessel immediately. The ship's crew pulled the mooring lines, and the ship moved away from the wharf. People standing on the wharf were waving, whistling, and shouting out to passengers on the ship. As the ship turned and headed toward the open sea, people standing on the wharf began to go back into town and into the market, doing what they did best, buying and selling the products and produce from the land.

I settled down in the economy class with the other people who were traveling to the capital. I sat next to an old man who was traveling to the capital city to see his children and grandchildren. He said he wanted to see his grandchildren while he still could. He said his beautiful wife of forty-two years of wonderful and blissful marriage had passed away five years earlier from old age, and for some reason, he told me this story:

My wife passed away five years ago from old age. It was a difficult time for me. I loved her so much, more than she loved me. It was a good thing being married to a beautiful woman with values and standards. Every woman is beautiful in their own right. That was what my father told me. They are unique and distinct and irreplaceable. There is not a replica or duplicable version of a woman, any woman at all for that matter. The woman you see walking around, she is the only one like her in the world. No one else is like her at all.

One thing that made our marriage work was the roles we played. Roles make marriage easy. Roles simplify marriage. There is no need for too much talking because the roles are clear. And when the roles are clear, it is smooth sailing. She knew what her responsibilities were, and I knew what my responsibilities were. They were founded on mutual respect and dependency. There was an appreciation for equal contribution to the well-being of our family. That is how marriage worked in my generation, young man. It might change dramatically in your generation.

In my generation, choosing a soulmate was based on character and values. There were certain qualities the significant other had to possess to qualify for marriage. You couldn't just pick someone based on her outward appearance. You had to check her background and the stock she came from, her family. I am nervous that it might all change in the years ahead. In the decades ahead, it might not be based on character or values or roles, but on something else, something superficial and temporary. So you will probably have to find another way to make a marriage work in your generation, if the roles are cancelled and not based on values anymore. That's the challenge and reality you are facing in the years ahead.

Respect is another issue of concern. Respect for parents or elders in the community or to anybody at all is a divine imperative. It sets you up for success in your future endeavors. People will make referrals about you in the community and say that you are a good man, a man of principle and integrity. It makes your life shine. You will be praised and openly talked about by people. Respect is never a given. It must be earned. It's the law of reciprocity. The most important discipline of all is self-discipline. If you cannot have self-discipline, then you cannot have discipline at all. Self-discipline is supreme. Self-discipline is the foundation for every other discipline. They are interrelated.

I also have a good relationship with my kids. But when they disobey instructions, I sit them down and tell them the consequences of their behavior, and the path it is taking them on if they don't stop. And too often, it is a path of frustration, pain, and regret. I cannot compromise on discipline in my family. My wife and I agreed on that when we first got married. We made it clear that discipline was number one when it came to our kids. We both were responsible for the discipline of the children," the old man continued.

We could not negotiate or debate or discuss discipline. Discipline was for application, not for negotiation. We always explained to them why we disciplined them, and after applying discipline, we prayed with them. We also taught them the benefits of obedience to parents or to instructions. It was for their benefit in the future. What we told them might have seemed uncomfortable in the moment, but it prepared them for the future. As parents, we are dispensable. We are not going to be around all the time. One day, we will be gone. And when we're gone, then it is in their hands to handle life without us.

To strongly affirm the reason behind discipline and its importance, I went further and made an appointment with the police officer in charge of prisons. I told him that I wanted to bring my family for a tour of the prison, so they could see firsthand the result of disobedience to their parents as the authority in the home. I wanted them to talk to the prisoners themselves. I wanted this to be an educational visit. The officer in charge accepted my request, and we booked the date. When I told my wife and kids about the visit, they were shocked. I told them it was all organized and there was nothing to worry about.

We arrived and the officer greeted us. We were given thirty minutes. He walked us through the hallway, showing us and telling us which prisoner lived in which room and how much time were they serving. As we paraded through, the prisoners looked through the small openings in their rooms and yelled out to my kids, "Young man! Young girls! Kids! Please stay out of trouble. Listen to what your father says! Listen to him; a father knows best. We don't want you kids to come here. This is a terrible place!"

As we kept walking, the officer opened the one man's cell. He had been there for about twenty-three years. His name was Mr. Amos Balili. My kids shook his hands, and he wept. He hugged all my kids and cried. He told my kids to listen to me and my wife.

"You know, kids, daddy knows best. I wish I had listened to my father. I am here because I disobeyed my father's instructions, the authority in the home. When you disobey authority, this is where you are going to end up. This is your destination. You don't need to end up here to taste the results of disobedience. In here, you never see the light of day nor the rainbow or the stars in the sky at night. You are a dead man in prison, the living dead. It's an awful place," Mr. Balili said. "Do you have a relative in prison serving jail time?"

"No, this is an educational visit for my kids. I want to show them where they will probably end up if they disobey authority or instructions," I explained.

"Oh man, I applaud you for taking that very important step," Mr. Balili said.

"When they think of breaking the rules or questioning my discipline, I want them to remember the consequences and where they are going to end up if they willfully choose to proceed," I said.

"You kids could help spread the word to other kids in your village and other villages nearby. They have seen firsthand a living cemetery," the prisoner said.

"So how many years have you been here now?" I asked him.

"I have been here for almost twenty-three years now. That's a long time. I wish I could just die now rather than live. It's pretty much the same to dying physically and being buried in a graveyard. In prison, you are the living dead," he said to me with his eyes welling up, choking back the tears. "Kids learn better when they actually see with their own eyes the end result of why you and your wife apply discipline at home."

On our way home in the truck, there was complete silence. No one was talking or saying a single word. It was like they were in a trance or had just finished watching a horror movie. They were spellbound, silent as dead men. They were so afraid, but it was a healthy fear. I told them a statement I heard one man say when he was pardoned by the crown. That man said, "Freedom is more precious than gold and silver. You never realize how valuable your freedom is until you lose it. No matter how much money or material possessions you amass or accumulate, they all mean nothing the very day you lose your freedom.

So as a father, I allowed my kids the freedom to do whatever they wanted, but first and foremost, I told them to think and weigh the outcome of the decisions they were about to make and see if it was worth taking the risk and losing their freedom. I don't want them to blame me as an authority in the home for not informing them. At least, I've given them the opportunity to see the result of disobedience to the discipline measures we apply at home. You know, kids learn fast and better when you show them what you have been telling them all along, especially when it comes to discipline. My kids never overstepped the boundaries we set after we visited the prison. Showing them the destination and the end result of disobedience made our jobs as parents easy, especially for me as a father.

We are literally training our replacements. We ensure that we left them trained and equipped to handle life and its challenges. That's why we applied discipline. We taught them discipline at breakfast, and at dinner before they went to sleep. It was repetition and a constant reminder of what is right and what is wrong, every single day.

Actually, after our prison visit, I did show them the beauty of obedience. I took the whole family again to a friend's home. This man was an ideal example of obedience to authority in the home. He emerged from humble beginnings, with both parents deceased when he was in boarding school. Through determination and hard work, discipline and curiosity, he was living a comfortable life. He reaped the rewards and benefits of obedience to instructions.

My kids really admired him. He traveled abroad every three months. He was neither rich nor poor. He was just financially comfortable. He applied the disciplines his father had taught him early on in life. He owned few real estate properties and two hundred and fifty beehives. Every two weeks, he would extract honey from the hives, and during harvest time when there was so much honey, he would get some people to help. He also owned three hundred laying chicken, supplying eggs to the shops in town. These money making mechanisms were not labor intensive.

They allowed and enabled him to spend time with his beautiful wife and kids. He often took his wife on a date on Thursday nights to rekindle his love and spark for his wife. They saw nobody on Thursdays. Thursdays were for him and his wife. It felt as if they were on their honeymoon all the time. He was still dating his wife, even though they had been married for thirty-five years and had three grown-up children. Sometimes, he would take her overseas for a date on a cruise ship. He never stopped dating his wife. He treated her like a precious jewel that he had found. There were photos of their cruise trips hanging on the wall. He was a different man. My kids admired how he lived his life, especially how he treated his wife with respect and dignity above all else. When it came to her happiness, she was his number one priority. He was living life on his terms." Just when I thought he could have stopped, he continued and raved on the fondest memories he shared with his deceased wife:

I remained single after my wife's passing. It was very hard sometimes. There used to be two cups on the table, but now only one; there were two plates at dinner time, but now one; our clothes hung on the line, but now just my old, rugged torn pants. Tea was cooked, hot and ready, when I got back from the bush on a hunting trip, but now I had to boil my own tea and cook my own food. It was cold under the sheets at night. There was no warmth or the feel of my wife in bed. It was different. It was strange. It was lonely. You have no one to share life with. It makes love incomplete again. There is no sharing. Love is not complete until you share it. It has meaning when you share it and give it away. It manifests in sharing and in giving.

But time does heal. I manage my own time and space. It is like when you are single, like you are right now, children. You don't need to be accountable or answerable to anyone with respect to how you utilize and manage your resources, especially your time. You don't have someone checking on where you're going and what you're doing. You literally have total freedom over how you want to live your life. That's the beauty of being single. You have more freedom. Embrace and enjoy your singleness; don't rush into loneliness. You are lonelier than when you are single if your marriage isn't working. Marriage is an institution of stress and loneliness if you don't know how to handle it. It is hell on earth.

People have this illusion that being married to someone will take away all their sorrows and troubles of being unmarried or single. Being married will amplify all your troubles and sorrows and expose who you really are. It will show your true colors when the winds of life blow and beat against that institution. Pressure manifests who we really are. It exposes the part of us that we are unaware of and don't want other people to know about. Pressure manifests our true self from the cocoon of deception that we have been hiding inside. If you want to know who you truly are, get married and stay with someone, and they will point out the flaws and the defects that you have been living with, unaware all along. You don't know how bad and stingy and selfish you are until someone is there to tell you.

Marriage is like trying to weld two pieces of iron together. The heat and the pressure are necessary to join the two into one. When they are fused, you cannot tell one from the other because they have finally become one. It is uncomfortable, but that is the process. You cannot get the desired outcome, which is a happy marriage, without going through the process of heat and pressures of life. When people fail to understand it from this perspective, they give up and walk away instead of sticking it through. The beauty of the heat and pressure is for two to become one.

My advice to you, a young man, is to enjoy your singleness. Don't rush into getting married. Figure out first what you want to achieve before you get married. Why? Because decision-making involves two, not one when you get married. Being single and independent and having it all together is proof that a man is ready to be married.

This old man was amazing. He loved to talk about things that mattered, unlike some old men that I came across. This one was totally different. He was insightful, captivating, and engaging. He was full of the kind of wisdom necessary to navigate the challenges of the times one is living in. I felt like I was sitting in a lecture theatre, listening to a talk on family and relationships. I felt like I was collecting nuggets at a mine site. The reservoir of wisdom this old man drew from was deep. Just when I needed to hear more, he continued:

Living with someone from a different background in a marriage covenant is a miracle. Waking up in the morning with her still sleeping beside you in one bed is a miracle. She could have run back to her parents' home during the night after figuring out you are not what you said you were, or her expectations and anticipations were met with disappointments. But what kept her in the bed, after finding out about everything, probably about all your lies and empty promises? It's the promise. The promise she made to you when she walked down the aisle, with her father holding her hand to give her away, into the hands of her new father, found in the knowledge and the declaration of these words "for better or for worse, for richer or for poorer, I promise I do, in sickness and *in health, I* will always love you," that's what kept her in the bed. It's the promise she made to you. Not feelings or emotions. It's the vow she made to you until death. If you can handle your singleness, you can handle your married life. Being independent is a prerequisite for marriage. And my last word to you is keep away from a woman until you are ready to awaken the beast within her. Her silent whisper and delicate touch will cause a mental distraction to reaching your destiny unless she is yours in a matrimonial covenant. She is the most powerful and deadliest creature to ever walk the planet.

Once she claws you, you are gone, you are finished. The best way to save your life is to run away as fast as you can. Don't negotiate or compromise or entertain her advances and sweet talk.

My advice to you, a young man, is to enjoy your singleness. Don't rush into getting married. Figure out first what you want to achieve before you get married. Why? Because decision-making involves two, not one when you get married. Being single and independent and having it all together is proof that a man is ready to be married.

As the ship approached the harbor, the old man went to the toilet and never returned. That's the last time I saw him.

Twenty minutes before docking, the captain announced, "Passengers, please make sure you take all your belongings with you. Check around for any rubbish and put it in the bin. On behalf of Coral Seas Shipping and the crew, I would like to thank you for traveling with us today. We hope your trip was a pleasant one, and we look forward to seeing you travel with us in the future."

# Chapter 3

# In Honiara, the Capital City, Lodging with the Sisters

I disembarked from the vessel and hailed a cab to take me to the sisters of the church residence. Sisters Mary Baitaburi and Martha Tagaai were living there. They never married by choice and had set apart their lives for the work of the ministry. They didn't want unnecessary distractions to interfere with the work they were doing. I walked up the hill to their house, my footfalls on the wooden steps. The lawn around the house was green and lush. It seemed to have been freshly mowed that morning, everything neat and green. It was a reflection of the clean and orderly living that the two sisters exhibited in every place they had lived. Wherever sisters of the church live, they keep it clean and lush as a tribute to their heavenly Father. You can tell the difference between sisters' abodes and those of regular people. It's the environment. The external environment is the reflection of a woman's heart and soul. Her goodness on the inside brings goodness to all that is around her.

I brought a bag of dry coconut and a bag of cassava to share with the sisters. I knocked on the door and Sister Martha opened the door, welcoming me into the house. Martha was always working in the kitchen.

"Hello, come on in. We heard that you would be coming today from Rebekah Warowaro, the registered nurse who works at White River clinic. How was the trip?"

"Awesome! The weather was magnificent, a perfect day for traveling on the ocean. Seagulls circling in sight and dolphins putting on a good show was breathtaking," I replied.

"That's good to hear. It's a pleasant day to go out in the reef, looking for clams and sea shells," Martha said. "Have a seat while I get you a glass of water. I will cook seafood for tea. I love seafood. I'll go and tell Sister Mary that you have arrived. She is pulling weeds and thistles from our small vegetable garden on the other side of the hill."

Both sisters returned quickly from the far side of the hill. "Hello Maduku, my name is Sister Mary Baitaburi. Nice to meet you. How was your trip?" Mary asked.

"The trip was awesome. I had good company on board, and it made me forget about the rigors of traveling," I said.

"What was the good company?" Mary probed with a smile.

"There was this old man, named Mr. Matthew Maalimae. We sat in the economy cabin with other passengers. My seat was next to him. For some reason, when the ship departed Auki wharf, he kept talking to me about his married life, the passing of his wife, and his concerns about marriage in the future. He fears that marriage won't be based on character and values in the decades ahead, but instead will be about personal interest and convenience. Listening to him talk made the journey exciting and the traveling bearable. It didn't feel like I was on the boat for as long as I had anticipated. The weather was magnificent. The sea was calm and friendly," I said.

"Wow! And where is the old man?" Martha asked.

"I lost him on the ship. He went to the toilet and never returned."

"People cross our paths for a reason. Embrace and cherish what he shared with you. It might spare you a lot of pain and heartache down the line," Mary said. "I'm done for the day. I will finish what I'm doing tomorrow."

"Sister Mary and I used to live in your area. We were nurses by profession back then and worked to combat leprosy, malaria, and tuberculosis. We were saddened to hear the deterioration of the clinic and its closure after our departure. The new administration was not doing enough to keep it operating and open to save lives. We conducted and coordinated cooking lessons, and taught the women about food, nutrition, and hygiene. We also taught the women how to take great care of themselves during pregnancy, prior to delivery and after the birth, making sure that mother and baby were healthy. We hope that one day, something good is going to emerge from that place again. Anyway, here is your towel, there is your room over there on the right, facing the ocean and the small stream. You know how to use hot water in the shower?" Martha asked.

"No, sister."

"No worries, I'll show you. First, you turn on the hot water, then you turn on the cold water. Turn them not too hot and not too cold, then you can have your shower. Be careful not to burn yourself in there," Martha called as she left me to my ablutions.

It was the first time that I had ever had a warm shower. I turned on the hot water first, then the cold one to balance the temperature. In the village, I usually just went to the river and swam in the cold water. It was chilly in the evenings, but you have no choice in the village. Sometimes, there was no soap or shampoo, and people would use red clay as soap.

I finished showering, dressed, and waited for the sisters at the dinner table, reading a newsletter about the work of other sisters around the country who had been doing similar work to what the sisters were doing. It was a quarterly edition that covered stories on food, nutrition, and hygiene to help people live healthier lives and make informed choices about the food they eat.

Dinner smelled delicious, and when it was served on the table, I grabbed a plate and helped myself. Sisters Martha and Mary joined in, each grabbing a plate each. "I love seafood! Thank you, Sister Martha, for cooking," Sister Mary said.

"You're welcome. There is an abundance of food here, Maduku. You can go back for seconds and thirds if you want, don't be shy," Martha said.

"So you won a scholarship to study overseas, right?" Mary asked.

"Yes, sister. Of the many who applied, I was the successful candidate chosen to study Human Resource Management. There are other successful candidates in other disciplines."

"Why you?" Mary continued her investigation.

"I think because of my superior academic performance. My grades were healthy. I have done exceptionally well in my exams and assessments. I worked hard in school. My aunt who raised me after my parents passed is a hard woman. She is hard on discipline and everything. And second, maybe, because I come from an underdeveloped area. The area I come from is often mocked and ridiculed for producing and contributing nothing towards the national economy of the country. If, however, it wasn't because of the area I come from, then it's definitely my marks that landed me the scholarship," I explained.

"Wow! Congratulations, you were granted a scholarship without paying a bribe."

"When I was little, I heard about the amount of money being allocated for development in my area, more than enough to build factories and plants to create jobs for the people, but the people have yet to taste the tangible benefits of that allotment because of mismanagement and greed. The international donor community is pumping more money into the country, and the amount of money exceeded the population of the country. There is more money than the number of men, women, and children combined. Yet, people are still waiting in limbo and groping to see the nation prosper and its citizens realize their dreams and aspirations materialize in real life. There is huge untapped potential in terms of resources, but it requires someone with a vision to get the job done. It needs someone audacious and competent to navigate the area I come from in its development, especially in industrial development," I said.

"How long are you going to study?"

"Three years."

"How do you feel about leaving home to go to college for the first time?"

"It's a bit daunting, but I'm excited. The feeling of leaving home and my people, and stepping into unfamiliar territory for the first time is nerve-racking. But I love exploring and stepping into uncharted waters. I believe great and amazing opportunities are waiting on the other side in the unknown. And in order to seize those precious opportunities, I have to leave the familiar and step into the unfamiliar"

"That's brave and courageous of you. Just bear in mind that you are a fine, handsome young man who can articulate well, especially when telling a story. Your narrative spin in telling a story is immaculate. Girls love a guy who knows how the story goes. They love to be entertained and taken on an adventure, a mentally and intellectually stimulating one. So your ability to communicate could work against you. I can tell by listening to you talk. Now I am a woman, and I love listening to you talk. As a woman, I relate to words on an emotional level. I feel them, I ruminate, and ponder upon them. So choose your words carefully before you say them, especially if you are talking with a woman because she feels and remembers every single word you say. She is like an incubator, an emotional one. Here is my analysis of you: You are a dangerous young man already. You have the ability to articulate and to inspire. If you are not careful, you will break many hearts." Mary said.

While Mary and I were talking, Martha was rinsing and cleaning the dishes in the sink. She agreed with what Mary was saying, about my ability to talk and inspire. If honed, polished, and harnessed properly, it could break many hearts for sure.

"Thank you very much for tea. That was delicious. I really enjoyed it,"

I said to the sisters.

"You are very welcome," Martha replied.

"When we were serving in your area, we often cooked and shared with the locals. They kept coming back to our kitchen because the food was free and delicious. You wiggled your toes while you were eating our food," Mary said. "We are great cooks. I guess, what kept them coming back was our cooking. We cooked with love. We put our heart and soul into everything we do when we are happy. So it's vitally important that our happiness is a priority and must not be taken for granted, whether we're in or out of the kitchen."

"You get unsatisfactory results when you don't give attention, appreciation, and affection for the woman and the food she cooks. It's really simple to make a woman happy. Just master the Triple A's, and she'll give you the world and everything in it, including the moon and the stars up in the sky. If you look at the triple A's, there's no mention of money, power, prestige or fame. It's all about her emotional needs. She cannot talk to money or a car or a house because she cannot relate to them on an emotional level. She needs warmth and touch. I think that is a good lesson to learn and master, my son, so that you know what to do when she comes into your life," Martha said. (The triple A's here are Affection, Attention and Appreciation)

"I appreciate that very much, especially, coming from a woman. Women know women better than men do," I said.

"So what is your aunt's occupation?" Martha asked.

"My aunt is a subsistence farmer. She works the land, growing vegetables, potatoes, cassavas, yams, and taro. She also raises a dozen pigs. I was the one assigned the task of feeding the pigs after school, before sunset every day. Now that I am gone, she must juggle gardening and feeding the pigs. I know she can handle it. She is a strong woman," I said.

"When we lived there, a pig was already a very expensive commodity. There was a high demand for pigs, but the supply was very low. People were willing to pay two to three thousand dollars for a pig. The demand was massive. But the people just raised pigs as a hobby. They didn't have the mindset to visual it as a money-making commodity. If one person just sees it differently and seizes the opportunity to shift from the seasonal and the hobbyist mentality, he would reap the benefits and the rewards big time. There are tons and tons of money to be made in pigs," Mary said.

"I told my aunt that raising pigs is so dear and close to my heart. I want to continue the tradition in the future and take it to the next level in a way it has never been done before. There is much wealth tucked away in a pig. What you said is very true. The good thing is that you don't need to invent pigs again. They have been on the earth since their discovery and appearance from generation to generation," I said. "The only hurdle and challenge is to shift from a casual mindset to a commercial one." "Exactly correct ." (I referred to the Bible tale of Noah's ark and all the animals. But I took out that line and replaced it with the line "They have been on the earth 'since their(pigs) discovery and appearance from generation to generation. Check to see if it harmonizes with the context of the text)

"So are you coming back home after college?" Mary asked.

"Listen, I'm an islander. I will rise and fall in the islands, and die and be buried in the islands amongst and with my own people. If I move and find work overseas, away from my people, then who would show them the way to move forward? They've have been waiting for so long. Their cries fall on deaf ears, and have been ignored for so long. No one cares anymore about their plight or their destiny. They are counting on me. I feel for my people. I lived with them, and what I saw made me sad and angry. I wanted to help, but I was helpless. They were like sheep without a shepherd. They don't know where they are going or how long they are going to wait. How long are we going to stand aside and see our natural resources being exploited right before our very eyes by greed and personal ambition? I believe there are alternatives available for better harvesting of our natural resources, but we are blind because nobody told us about them. I believe there is a better way, and we must find it. If all we care about is money, then one day, once our resources are exhausted, we will wake up to the reality that we cannot eat money."

"That's a very good point you just made. You cannot eat money once your natural resources are gone. Oh boy, you are so observant and analytical. I believe you will do well in your college studies," Sister Mary said.

"Well, it's past midnight. Let's call it a night. Tomorrow is Sunday. We will have brother Andrew Suumalefo joining us for lunch. We will have taro and pork for lunch, something different. Have a good night's sleep, Maduku," the sisters said. They left the dining table and disappeared into their rooms.

I lay on a five ply mattress. I never slept on a mattress in the village. Instead, I slept on a mat woven out of coconut fronds. Sleeping on a coconut frond mat was uncomfortable, but you had no choice, especially if you were a boy. Families who could afford a mattress gave it to the girls to sleep on. If you were a boy, and your family could not afford to get a mattress, a coconut frond mat was the next best thing they could afford to give you to sleep on.( I replaced home umbrella with coconut frond mat. It's a mat weaved out of coconut fronds/leaves).

Laying on the mattress in my room, I looked at the moon and the stars in the sky. The stars formed a wonderful, magnificent constellation. I could hear the waves splashing on the shoreline. I wanted to go down to the beach and sit in the moonlight. The feeling of the ocean breeze bristling on the skin was so tempting. But I was new in town, and I was scared that I might get bashed for money or something. Besides hearing the waves splashing on the shoreline, I could also hear the sound of toads croaking along the small stream beside the house. The moon's illumination that shone through the window was soothing and rejuvenating. It was possible to see an ant crawling on the ground in the moonlight. But I forced myself to go to sleep, and because I was weary after my long ocean journey, I slept through the night.

# Chapter 4

# Still In Honiara, the Capital City

Sister Mary usually woke up at four-thirty every morning to do some reading. She boiled tea and read the newsletter about the good works done by other sisters around the country. She also recorded her thoughts and reflections about what she had read in the newsletter. She loved journaling. There was a pile of more than forty journals on her bookshelf in her room. She recorded everything she was doing every day. She was committed and dedicated to journaling, never missing a single day to jot down her thoughts in her journal.

I woke up and went to join Mary in the living room.

"Oh, good morning. Did you have a good night's sleep?" Mary asked.

"Yes, I did" I replied.

"I usually wake up early to read and write in my journal," she said.

"What are you writing?"

"I am jotting my thoughts and reflections about what I read, and what I do each passing day during the week."

"What's the importance of journaling?" I asked. "I was never taught journaling in primary and high school."

"Well, there are many reasons that journaling is important, but there is one that came to my mind right now. It's about treasures that you are going to leave behind when you die, and one of my treasures is my journal. I don't have much money or material possessions or a house or car to leave or pass on to the next kin. So I'm going to leave my thoughts behind in a journal, hoping that someone might be inspired and motivated to keep pursuing their dreams regardless of where they come from or what they are going through or facing in life.

I want to leave information for the next generation to read and enjoy, and perhaps, learn about the world I am living in, my daily interactions and the conversations I have with people I meet on the streets, at church or at the market. My journal can tell the future about the world that we are living in now," Sister Mary said. "I am a quiet achiever. I don't preach my successes and achievements. I just want to be like a tree, bringing forth fruit without expecting anything in return."

"I never saw journaling that way. That's inspiring! I might start jotting down my thoughts, too, now that I realize the significance of journaling and why you are doing it. What an invaluable treasure to leave behind," I told her.

It was lunch time, and Martha had everything baked, cooked, hot, and ready. They were expecting brother Andrew Suumalefo to join them for lunch. He had devoted his life to the work of the ministry. It was twelve forty-five in the afternoon, and Mr. Suumalefo, dressed in brown shorts and a button shirt, walked up the wooden steps. His attire was decent and gentle. He took off his sandals and left them on the porch. He knocked on the door, and Sister Mary greeted him,"Hello, Brother Andrew! Come on in and grab a chair. This is our guest, Mr. Maduku Mamata. He arrived yesterday from his home island. He is leaving for college in two weeks."

"Hello, Maduku. I'm brother Andrew Suumalefo. Nice to meet you, buddy"

"Nice to meet you, too."

"He was granted a scholarship to study Human Resource Management at college for three years, everything paid for," Mary continued.

"Wow, congratulations man! That's awesome!" Andrew said. "A prestigious and coveted scholarship like that demands convincing and an exceptional grade point average," Andrew exclaimed.

"You are exactly correct. I scored good marks on my exams. My grades are healthy. I studied, worked hard, and spent a lot of cruel hours chewing through my books and notes under a hurricane lantern. And also, I was chosen perhaps because of the area that I come from. It is underdeveloped, and has been that way for well over four decades. There is no development happening. It is dormant and static. There are natural resources in abundance, but the necessary machinery and technology is missing," I said.

"I believe you are the answer to the cries of your people in your area. You are the answer to their prayers, that beacon of hope when it's cold, dark, and lonely. Things like that are not coincidental. They are predetermined by the universe. You are that seed of hope they have been waiting on to germinate and spring from the earth. You see, when life shows you a problem, life is telling you to find a solution because no one else is seeing it besides you. When you see an injustice in the world and it makes you angry, that is life telling you to do something about the very thing that angers you.

You became responsible the very moment you saw it and understood it. If you ignore and turn a blind eye to it, you will lay on your death bed, about to cross over, the ghost of that situation or problem standing beside you with large angry eyes, blaming you for not doing something, or finding the solution, or making that situation better for humans and the world. When we see it from that perspective, then we begin to organize and take responsibility and do something.

It makes us obligated and responsible. I think you are a responsible young man because you are the one who saw the urgency and understood what is lacking in your area. When you feel obligated to do something about a particular situation for the good of humanity and the world, life begins to do business with you. I can't wait to hear of the amazing things that you are going to achieve after college. I want to read your story and your history," Mr. Suumalefo said.

"Thank you so much. It warms my heart to hear words of hope and courage from people like you. I deeply appreciate that so much."

"We lived and worked in the district he comes from almost three decades ago. After our departure, the good work we started died because of poor management and irresponsibility of the new administration. It saddens our heart to hear that what we put our heart and soul into just went down the drain. The closure of the clinic that we used to work at is the worst thing that could have happened," Sister Mary said. "But I remain optimistic that one day, something good is going to emerge from that area."

While Mary was talking with me and Andrew, Martha was in the kitchen, sorting food into different bowls and trays. She never complained because Mary was not helping. She hummed a tune while going about her jobs. When the food was all sorted, she brought it to the table. Brother Andrew got up from his chair and lent Martha a hand, bringing the food to the table. The scent of the food was tantalizing to my taste buds.

"Alright, everybody, food is ready. Grab a plate and help yourself. Thank you, Brother Andrew, for joining us. We really appreciate your being here. You and Maduku have made this afternoon different. There is more food in the kitchen. So don't be shy," Martha said.

Brother Andrew opened his heart to us during that meal. He shared many things with me and the sisters:

I have been to many places, at home dend abroad. I love adventure. I love sightseeing, visiting new places, and talking to amazing people who have done great things for their communities. They are the unsung heroes we never hear about outside our borders. They help transform their communities into vibrant places to live by serving their gifts and talents with gratitude and a willing heart to help. Community service is the fuel that keeps them going. They paint their portrait through the work that they do. They work tirelessly and selflessly to make their communities vibrant, strong, and effective. They are full of energy and drive. They have a strong zest for living. You can only meet them when you travel outside your known world. Exposure to the outside world is a good thing. It broadens your scope and your horizons. It's also an opportunity to observe and learn about how people do things and why they do it, then come back and implement those things in their communities to achieve similar results.

My profession as a counselor is a rewarding experience. I am constantly learning about human beings. Very complicated creatures. I graduated with a diploma in counseling from Bethel College of Evangelism. Being a counselor for almost two decades now has taught me much about the complicated issues people face and grapple with in their personal lives or marriages. Every new case demands a solution at a different level. You have to take into consideration many factors to decipher the cause and the remedy to the problems.

I am humbled by the privilege afforded me by the people I have offered counseling to over the years. They allowed me to delve into their worlds to decipher the root of a certain issue they face in their lives. For people in relationships, sometimes the cause of an issue just requires a slight change in priorities. When the priorities are neglected, it grows into an unnecessary issue. I love my job. It challenges me to hone and sharpen my ability to discern meaning by listening and paying careful attention when people are talking and opening up. And I am constantly learning to hone my craft by reading books about positive psychology and other genres. I discovered that the more you apply what you learn in real life, the more it opens up new dimensions and streams you have never traveled or explored before.

I also encounter lonely people, especially those who are trapped in a relationship that isn't working. They put on a good face in public, pretending that it is smooth sailing. But all the while, they are going through a silent hell. Nothing is worse than being in a relationship that isn't working. It is hell on earth. You are single right now, and so you don't know loneliness. *You don't know what it feels like when two people, a man and a woman sleep in the same room, back to back, and never talk.*

They come home from work at different times, just to avoid one another. They walk past each other in the hallway and are afraid to say something because there could be a fight. The stress level is high, and it's draining. You are single. Enjoy your singleness. Don't rush into getting married. Score those big and important goals first. It is easier when you are single. When you are single, you manage your own time, space, money, friendships without being accountable to anyone. But when you are married, you can no longer do whatever you feel like doing. You cannot just buy anything you feel like buying. You need to consult your spouse for approval. Decision-making takes two now, not one like when you were single.

This is the advice I give to young people when I have the chance to talk to them. I am trying to save them the problem, the heartache, and the stress of not rushing into a relationship. I tell them to slow down and work on themselves to be the best they can be. So when they give themselves to someone, they are giving something valuable that can add meaning to the other person's life.

"Brother Andrew, you have impacted my life so much. It's great to meet you. Meeting you during this lunch hour was not a mistake. It was meant to be so I could draw from your experience as a guide to where I am going in my life. While you were talking, you reminded me of an old man I met on the ship yesterday. He shared similar sentiments to what you said. He told me about his personal life, before his marriage and after his wife's passing. The pearls of wisdom you both dispelled are priceless," I said to him.

"So you are leaving for college in a fortnight?" Andrew asked.

"Sister Martha will take me to the Embassy to pick up the visa application forms tomorrow," I explained.

"Very good. Thank you so much for lunch, sisters. Mary and Martha, that was delicious. I enjoyed it and am now extremely full. I probably don't need to cook tea tonight. And I think I should go now. Someone is coming to see me around three o'clock. Nice meeting you, Maduku. I hope to meet you again someday. You take care, and all the best in your college studies," Andrew said.

Andrew left the sisters' residence with a sense of satisfaction. He had poured out a bit of himself in sharing information with me that would probably help him to stay on course in his college studies. Speaking to young people was something that was near and dear to his heart. He always availed himself to speak to young people, giving them his time and attention. He had seen so many talented young men and women fall through the cracks because of neglect and a lack of good information. He had made it his life's mission to reach out to as many young people as he could because the future belonged to them. They were the next bearers of the baton.

"Tomorrow, I want you to come with me to the market. We will do a bit of shopping. I need you to help carry the shopping bags for me. Then on Tuesday, we'll go to the embassy to pick up the application forms to apply for your student visa," Martha said. "Mary will continue doing what she was doing, clearing and pulling the weeds from the vegetable garden on the other side of the hill. I will cook tea for us tomorrow evening, lobsters and mud crab. I have a craving for them as it has been a while since I tasted both."

On Monday, Martha and I arrived at the market early in the morning. I was surprised to see truckloads and boatloads of local produce being unloaded. They came from the four corners of the island. Some came on pickup trucks, some come by outboard motor boats, and some by ship.

"This is the central market. It is the central hub for fishermen and farmers to display their catch and produce," Martha said. "Carvers and sculptors sometimes come here to display their crafts, too. When you think of fresh and locally-grown organic food, look no further. The central market has it all in one place. You will also notice some interesting folks, sitting idly, killing time watching the people buying and selling. For some reason, they leave home early in the morning, too, like those who go to work. But they just come to the market and sit at the corner. They go home at the same time the working folks go home. That's sad. They should have found something worthwhile to do, like grow some vegetables and come sell them at the market. I think they don't want to put in the effort." Martha looked at the people on the corner and sighed.

While they were looking at some fresh vegetables, a woman from the crowd called out Martha's name. "Sister Martha, come over here!"

Martha turned and saw it was Elizabeth Okamola, a widow with three kids. "Hey Elizabeth, how are you?"

"I'm good, I'm good, Sister Martha."

"Long time no see. How are the kids doing?"

"The kids are doing fine, two in school and the last born is here with me. It's tough and challenging raising three kids and putting them through school as a single mom. But if you are determined to give them a better future, you have no excuses whatsoever. You don't complain and start blaming other people and the society. You take responsibility instead."

"Oh girl, you sound brave and courageous and inspirational. You go, girl! Actually, a determined woman is invincible in whatever she desires to accomplish in life," Sister Martha said.

"I want the best for my kids. I want them to be successful and live life on their own terms," Elizabeth replied quietly.

"I admire the resilient spirit in you, Elizabeth. Your attitude and zest for living are amazing. You don't know how many women you have inspired out there, and they are watching you in secret. You're not thinking of finding love again?"

"My doors are open, but I'm not desperate or rushing into settling down anytime soon. It's lonely and cold, but as women, you know, we are armed and equipped to get the job done, you know," she winked.

"I know, I know, my dear sister," Martha smiled.

"Warmth and touch are essential. I missed out on a lot, but a girl always finds her way through the maze in the woods," Elizabeth said.

"Beautifully put, my dear," Martha said. "So what are you selling?"

"Bananas and Avocados."

"I love avocados. They are nutritious, and they're great for your skin," Martha said.

From under the concrete table, Elizabeth grabbed a green basket woven of coconut fronds, packed full with bananas. She filled a plastic bag with the beautiful bananas. Then she reached into a brown box full of avocados. She filled another plastic bag with avocados and gave it to Sister Martha. "Take this home. Say hello to Sister Mary for me and the kids."

"I will definitely do that. Thank you so much, Elizabeth. If you ever miss the truck to go home after selling your products, just head up to our residence on the hill. You know where we live. By the way, this is our guest, Maduku. He is leaving for college soon. Sister Mary and I used to work in his district a while ago. It's great and inspiring to see young lads pursuing higher education."

"That's the path I want my kids to follow. I want them to live life on their terms."

"Tomorrow, we will pick up his visa application forms at the embassy. Today, I asked him to follow me to do some shopping," Martha further explained.

"It's so nice to see you again, Martha. I always come here on Mondays," Elizabeth said. "Come on down to the market on Mondays. I will always be here if the weather permits."

"Alright, darling. Nice talking with you. We better keep it moving."

I walked with Martha over to where the fishermen had their stands. Fresh tuna and snapper fish were on display, and lobsters were stored in a cooler filled with ice cubes to keep them fresh. About fifteen mud crabs were displayed on the floor with their legs tied. A fisherman gave us a snapper fish for free. Martha reached for her purse and insisted that she should pay for it, but the man told her that he wouldn't accept her money.

We bought six pounds of lobsters and five mud crabs. A man and his son were selling the mud crabs. They gave us one mud crab for free, a total of six mud crabs altogether, including the donated one. "Some generous people are in the marketplace, too, Maduku," Martha said. My hands were full with two plastic bags of lobsters and mud crabs. "It's time to go home now. Let's walk to the taxi bay," she continued.

We left the market building and walked to the taxi bay. The city mayor drove by, and seeing them, turned around at the roundabout and came to a stop at the taxi bay.

"Where are you two going? Jump in, I'll take you home," he said.

"No, we are fine. We can get a cab home," Martha replied. But he insisted and we got into his car. (Replace car with Hilux. They hopped into his Hilux)

"I am the mayor of the city. I just returned from a meeting at Sunset Hotel. Where are you going to?"

"You know the sisters' of the church residence on the hill?"

"Oh, I know where you live. Were there many people at the market today?" he asked.

"A lot of people, which is a bit weird for a Monday," Martha said.

Later as we drove, the mayor, a man of great wisdom, began to talk.

"I go shopping with my wife on Saturdays. She loves shopping. When she reaches the floral section, we stand there for hours. I never complain. I just roll with her. Twice a week, I buy her flowers for no reason. I love her so much and tell my friends publicly that I would crawl over broken glass to get to her, and if she leaves me, I'm going with her. Her happiness is supreme and a priority for me.

"Together, we are currently reaching out to the youth in the village. We go home on a quarterly basis. My heart is for the youth, the next generation. We started a vegetable project and provided the resources for the project with our own money. We don't ask for donations. These days, people are tired of being asked for money to start something. So my wife and I funded the project with our own finances. It doesn't cost much. We believe in managing what little we have, and over time, the returns will come back multiplied many times.

"We engaged five young people to tend to the garden. We gave them clothes to wear. We helped them open savings accounts at the bank. We also built a house for one of the five boys, a standard semi-permanent one. The roof is thatched, with flooring and walls made of timber. We mounted a 10 watts solar power tile to the roof, just for lighting at night. For cooking, he uses firewood. It's attracting attention and making news in the area. It's something that has never happened before.

"To my wife and I, it seemed like the forgotten and the neglected were beginning to hatch out from the cell of conventional wisdom, and if you don't challenge the status quo or if you don't have an educational degree, you cannot maximize your potential and reach your destiny in life. One thing I figured out and learned in this process is that the best time to rise and shine is in the midst of confusion and disillusionment. Don't whine, but get busy and start working. Complaining never improves anything, never ever. People who complain a lot are the problem. There is a difference between complaining and constructive criticism. The latter is for improvement and progress. The former is toxic and offers nothing for growth and development.

"The turnover from the sales is divided and distributed equally into the accounts of the five young people after setting aside running money and money for investing. That's the model we created because right now, people are confused. There is too much talk and too little action. So many good ideas just died and are covered in dust on office desks and cabinets. They sound so good on paper but aren't compelling enough, and the people behind them lack a personal conviction that is stronger than death to propel those ideas into fruition. That's why we aren't seeing much progress.

"So besides being the mayor of the city, that's what my wife and I are doing. We are investing in the next generation. We are looking into expanding and reaching out to the youth in other villages in the future. The model is easily duplicated. It only needs a few who understand it and start implementing it rather than waiting on people to pour in money. Now the people in my village believe that everyone achieves more when they work together. We are ready to give a hand to youth who want change and meaning in their lives."(Still the mayor's piece)

Now, what about the gentleman in the back, what is he doing? Is he visiting, or helping with something, or your houseboy?(Still the mayor's piece, he's asking a question to sister Martha)

"Oh, no," Martha said. "This gentleman is leaving for college in a fortnight. He was granted a three-year scholarship to study Human Resource Management. We are going to the embassy tomorrow to pick up the forms for his visa."

"Congratulations, young man! We need more young people like you, pursuing higher education overseas," the Mayor exclaimed. "That's the path I want the boys who we are looking after to travel. They were dropouts from primary school. It warms my heart to hear young men like you traveling on a high road to higher education. I look forward to seeing you in a position of responsibility when you come back to serve our country. All the best in your future endeavors."

We arrived at the sisters' residence and hopped out. "Thank you so much, Mayor, for the lift," Martha said.

"Not a problem. It was my great pleasure. All the best in college, young man." And he disappeared like smoke around the bend.

We walked up the steps to find that Mary had finished clearing weeds in the little veggie garden and was waiting for us to arrive. Taking the two plastic bags off my arm, Mary put them on the table. "How was the shopping?" she asked.

"Oh, it was fantastic. We encountered generous and kind-hearted people today. The mayor of the city gave us a lift home," Martha replied.

"What! You mean the mayor of the city gave you two a lift home?"

"Yes, he did. He saw us at the taxi rank, turned at the roundabout and pulled up at the taxi bay," Martha said.

"That speaks volumes and is surprising, really," Mary said. "The mayor is a very busy man. He picked you two up because he saw a sister or something."

"I don't know, but he did give us a lift home today," Martha said.

"He's a good bloke with a big heart. He told us a bit about what he and his wife are doing for the youth in his village. It's inspiring listening to his vision. I was sitting in the back listening to every single word he said. It seems every person I bump into has something to tell me. The old man on the ship, Brother Andrew Suumalefo, and the city mayor. All three said pretty much the same things. It's a divine coincidence," I said.

Martha sat down at the table, looking at our day's purchases. "You might think it's coincidental but it's not. When you cross the path of perfect strangers and they touch your life in unexplainable ways, embrace and treasure what they say. It's fuel for the journey," Mary said. "Your journey may be long, and you might not get there as quickly as you expected. So you need to carry extra fuel in your reserve because the road is not always even. It's good to reach your destination and still have fuel left over because you will always be going places after you've arrived. Don't ask for security, but ask for adventure. Don't be satisfied with your present accomplishments. Even if you have achieved your goal, start working on another one. By doing that, life will be worth living and fun. If you achieved something and it didn't kill you, it simply means that there is so much still left on the inside.

"Always stay hungry and curious, refusing and rejecting the temptation to remain static or stagnant or satisfied with your past accomplishments. That is frozen success. And as a young learner, you should have two big ears and one small mouth. But when you grow older, you should have two small ears and one big mouth.

"Always listen and ask questions when you interact and mingle with accomplished people. They probably have something to tell you. One piece of advice I want to share with you is this: Never ever graduate from the *life school of learning* because all you know is what you have learned, and what you have learned is *never* all there is to know. No matter what you know, there will still be things that you don't know. So develop that attitude of curiosity, hunger, and thirst for knowledge like a deer that pants for the water brooks.

"Absorbing knowledge is like letting rays of light shine through a dark room, driving and pushing away the darkness that is ignorance. You know, ignorance is simply choosing to stay unaware of something that is readily available all along in your environment, like a person or a book. The answer that we need to help solve a particular situation we are dealing with might be found in the person living next door or in a book collecting dust on the bookshelf in our homes. Our personal ego and the pride of not seeking help from the resources that are available, fearing that we might be mocked, ridiculed, or perceived as unintelligent, often hinders and slows us down from getting to our destinies as quickly as we hoped."

Sister Mary didn't contribute much to intellectual conversations or sharing of thoughts and personal reflections about the world they were living in. She looked after the kitchen and ensured that there was food in the pantry. She loved to cook and go to the market to buy food. She loved shopping and collecting stuff to pile up and feast her eyes on in the house. She was different from Martha. She ensured that her guests were being looked after and wanted to be remembered as an excellent host.

It was Tuesday morning, the second day of a new week. Martha and I went to the embassy to pick up forms for my visa application. We arrived and was greeted by a beautiful Caucasian lady. She had an easy smile with blue eyes and blonde hair. She had the form and looks of a model. Her waist curved like a guitar. Her legs were slender and sleek, so captivating to look at. Her lips were red with lipstick but her dress code was formal and decent, not revealing.

"Good morning, how can I help you?" She had an infectious smile.

"Good morning, how are you doing?" Martha asked in return.

"Not too bad, thank you."

"Here is this gentleman's letter of admission to study Human Resource Management at St Andrew's college. His name is Mr. Maduku Mamata." Martha could see her name written on a tag, Ms. Julia Adams. "What else do we need to provide, Ms. Adams?"

She looked at the admission offer and picked out a few forms from the desk drawer and gave them to us. "Get these forms and fill in Maduku's personal details and bring them back to me for submission. Leave the admission offer here with me. If you could bring the forms back on Thursday, that would be great, so I can lodge the application as quickly as I can. Come back in here on Thursday. If I'm not here, just drop it in this box."

We took the forms, thanked Ms. Adams, and left the embassy. When we arrived home, we looked through the forms. We put in my personal particulars, address and contact details. For the residential address, we just used the sisters of the church address. We showed Sister Mary the forms. She read through them and gave them back to us.

"The lady at the reception said if we're unsure about any question in the forms, she will help us fill them in," I said.

"That's so kind of her. She's a good girl by the sound of it," Mary said.

On Thursday, Martha and I took the application forms back to the embassy. When we arrived, Ms. Adams was there. We handed her the forms and she opened the envelope and took a quick look at them. Then she nodded and said, "Excellent, I will write down the college address for you. Just write your names and sign your signatures here. Then you are free to go. Check back Thursday next week for the outcome."

When Martha and I arrived home, Mary asked, "How did things go with you two today?"

I offered, "We handed the forms to the lady. She said to check back on Thursday for the outcome. It might take a week or so for processing."

"That's good," Mary responded, smiling.

"Tomorrow I will be visiting the children's ward at the hospital," Martha said. "Would you like to come with me, Maduku?"

"Sure, I would like to accompany you to the hospital," I replied.

Friday morning came around. I put on something nice to walk the distance to the hospital from the sisters' residence. I carried a box of goodies—cricket balls, balloons, tennis balls, soccer balls, teddy bears, and some storybooks to read to the children. As we entered the entrance to the hospital, an ambulance arrived and stopped in front of the emergency room. Someone had been badly wounded from knife cuts because of a tribal dispute over logging. He was placed on the stretcher and rushed to the emergency room. Martha, for some reason, made a statement that I will never forget as long as I live.

"One day, when all the trees are gone, people will discover that they cannot eat money. That notion applies to all the other resources as well. There are renewable and environmentally sound and friendly resources in abundance. It just needs some organizing to extract and convert them into cash in a sustainable fashion," she said. "This is the fourth time this year that someone has been hurt and rushed to the hospital over a logging dispute. It's sad that greed and personal ambition prevail over sharing and caring for each other in the distribution of wealth that accrues from the extraction of natural resources."

We arrived at the children's ward. A novice nurse greeted us with a firm handshake, a big infectious smile, and a laugh. She had just graduated from college with a diploma in nursing. "Good morning sister, how are you doing?"

"I'm doing pretty well, thank you. This is Maduku. He is my guest and is lodging with me and Sister Mary. He is leaving to study at St Andrew's college shortly, and he is waiting for his visa to be granted. We dropped off his visa application forms yesterday. I asked him to come with me for a visit today to see the children."

"Good morning, brother, nice to meet you. I'm Naomi Fefenu. I am doing my probation at the moment. I just graduated from college last

November. Come on in for a chat, and thanks for visiting me and the kids today."

Martha and I followed Nurse Fefenu. She gave us vests to wear with the word 'Visitor' written on the back. She walked with us through the ward, as we distributed the goodies to each sick child. The toys put a big smile on the children's faces. It made the day better and better as I could see that it really lifted their spirits. After distributing the goodies, we sat down with Nurse Fefenu at her desk and chatted about experiences working with sick kids. Her supervisor was away, running an errand in town.

While we were talking, the nurse was very keen to ask me some questions. She asked about my goals and dreams for the future, and what I wanted to do after college. She also asked if I was involved. She maintained eye contact with me during the entire conversation, which made me feel a bit weird, but I was innocent and didn't know what to think about it.

Sister Martha, however, was a grown up woman, and she knew that Nurse. Fefenu's intentions were not honorable. She could tell by looking at her eyes, which were full of lustful desire. She often giggled without reason when I was talking. The way she looked at me said it all. Unbeknownst to me and my naive ways, she liked me, but Sister Martha knew what was going on. As a woman, she could tell by Nurse Fefenu's body language that she really liked me.

As we were about to leave the hospital, she kissed me on the cheek and said, "Thank you for visiting, handsome. You are one cute cat. Not many young people would do what you did, visiting sick kids. I hope to see you again in the future. The girl who is going to marry you one day is a very lucky girl, and I wish I was that girl." She laughed loudly. Sister Martha and I looked at each other in disbelief.

"Don't get nervous about it, I'm just thinking out loud," she said laughing and patting and rubbing my back. It seemed she couldn't handle herself. "Thank you, Sister Martha, for visiting today. I hope you will visit again soon."

"For sure, darling," Martha said and gave her a hug. "You are so excited today I can tell."

"Of course I am. I don't know why."

"I know," Martha said laughing. They both laughed at themselves. Sister Martha and I left soon afterward.

We exited the hospital's premises. I thought about the kiss from the nurse, and my heart began to beat quite quickly. The nurse was a gorgeous and kind-hearted girl who was ready to take on life with all its challenges, but she was very busy with work and had no time to go out socializing. I couldn't believe that I just been kissed by a very beautiful lady who was a nurse and a college graduate.

Knowing that I was still thinking about the kiss from the nurse, Sister Martha eased my nerves by saying, "You know, Maduku, when a girl kisses you in the way she did, it means that she likes you. There is something about you that captures her heart. I can tell that she liked you very much. The look in her eyes was different, not the usual look. She did not hide her feelings towards you. She was open and vulnerable, and it was obvious and undeniable by her behavior when she was around you.

"When a girl likes a man, she doesn't muck around in showing it," she continued. "She doesn't care who's watching. In a crowd or alone, she will make it known with a kiss or a hug within a few seconds of her deadly stare. She doesn't hesitate to express her feelings to the person she admires and adores. I saw something else in her eyes. Her eyes started welling up and were drawn with strong emotions. It was a strong and powerful message that she liked you so much. No doubt about it. I have never seen or met someone so obsessed like that in my entire life."

After we left the children's ward, the nurse couldn't concentrate on her job. She couldn't finish her shift properly. She told her supervisor that she needed some rest and wanted to go home. There was so much going on inside her head. Eventually, her supervisor released her to go home and have a rest.

# Chapter 5

# Still In Honiara, the Capital City

The next Thursday, Sister Martha and I went back to check on the outcome of the application. We walked in and the gorgeous lady was there, looking like a model. "Good morning, how are you doing?"

"Not bad at all," Sister Martha said with a smile.

"I have good news for you, Mr. Mamata. I am thrilled to inform you that your application has been assessed, and a student visa has been granted. You must pick up your plane ticket at the national airline's office, and organize yourself to leave the country on the date stated on the ticket," she said. Then she looked at me and noticed a sense of nervousness in my eyes. She thought it would be good if she could offer me some comfort and ease my fears. She wanted to tell me about her personal experience and discovery about college study.

Sir, if you don't mind, I want to share with you a few things regarding college and the myths about college study. I just recently graduated from college with a BA in Public Administration. Initially, I thought college was like high school or something, where the teacher is in the class the whole time, answering questions and clearing up the student's confusion, but it's not. At college, the professor is just a resource. During my time there, my professor was a male. He came into the class, introduced himself and the course of study for the semester for about ten to fifteen minutes, and then he left. He told us to read a few chapters and write a report about what we had read.

From that moment on, it dawned on me that I was literally paying an institution to tell me to go read a book at the library and write a paper. That's what a college is. You pay the institution, and they give you books to read. Then at the end of your study, they give you a certificate or a diploma or a degree to certify that you have done a course with the school and satisfied the requirements. So my experience taught me that when you go to college, like you are going to do shortly, your sponsors are paying for you to study. Actually, they are paying for you to read books.

We are not disciplined enough to read books by ourselves, so we pay someone to make us go to the library and read, and that is called college. When you go to college, you go to get ideas, and then they certify you when you reach a certain number of ideas. It's called a certificate or a diploma. That's my personal experience and discovery. You go and find out and write to me if your findings and experience are different. Ideas are so powerful that we have to pay an institution to make us read them. And what are in those books? Ideas.

Some people whose ideas we read are already dead, and they speak from their graves to us through their ideas left behind in a book. Some are still living. You might want to say that the world is ruled by the dead. They rule from their graves through their ideas because their ideas outlived them. And the challenge for us who are alive is to decide what we are going to leave behind when we die, something that could outlive us and speak to the next generation. Think about that for a while.

But the attractive part of college, if you are sponsored, is the student allowance. I was fortunate to save a substantial amount of my allowance for my future wedding. I lived with very little. I did not go out to eat or clubbing on the weekends. I saved, and I saved, and I saved. I could not believe how much money I had saved at the end of my study. You can do the same if you want to. You can save money and build a house or start a business after you finish college.

With respect to the course of study, it is entirely on your shoulders. The professor is just a resource. Whether you graduate or not is up to you, not the professor. You are the one who is going to do the work. You will be required to do a comprehensive reading of books in your field of study because you are contributing to a body of knowledge. You are going to put in a lot of cruel hours by delving into the books. I hope what I share with you will ease and clear your fears and confusions. But generally, college is good, especially if everything is paid for, as it is in your case. All you have to do is read and write. I like the social environment it creates. It helps you to forge lasting friendships with people from different backgrounds and walks of life. You will also create fond memories that will last a lifetime.

"Thank you so much, thank you very much for demystifying the myth about college study. It was daunting, but now I feel confident and at ease. Your experience is a good one, and I appreciate that so much. Thank you," I said. "You are welcome."

Sister Martha and I left the embassy feeling ecstatic. On the way home, we talked about what Ms. Adams had said to me, how kind-hearted she had been in sharing her college experience and how good that she had managed to save money for her future wedding from the student allowance.

"She possessed good people skills, and her fluency in articulating what's on her mind is amazing. She is gorgeous with the form and the looks of a model, an ideal figure for a magazine cover or something," Martha said. I readily agreed.

We went to the national airline's office at the airport to pick up my ticket. The airline officer was a beautiful woman with dark pigmentation.

Her face and legs were shiny and smeared with coconut oil. "Good morning, how can I help?"

"Good morning, how are you doing?" Sister Martha said.

"Not bad, thank you."

"We are here to pick up this gentleman's ticket."

She printed the ticket and handed it to me. "Congratulations, young man, and all the best in your future endeavors."

"Thank you so much."

"No worries. Have a safe and enjoyable trip."

# Chapter 6

## Still in Honiara, the Capital City

Meanwhile, the nurse did not manage to finish her shift as she did every other day. She wasn't focused and concentrated. She told her supervisor that she needed some rest, and because her supervisor was an understanding bloke, he allowed her to go home early. She left the hospital, feeling weak and drowsy.

She crossed the road to catch her bus. Many people were waiting at the bus stop. The bus stopped, and she boarded. She sat close to the window, resting her head against the glass screen, her eyes closed. The conductor tapped her shoulder to ask for her bus fare. She gave him two dollars and fifty cents and closed her eyes again. "Wake me up at the bus stop opposite the market near the sea," she said to the conductor.

"Not a problem, I will," the conductor said.

The bus reached her stop, and the conductor woke her as she had requested. Wiping the sleep from her eyes, she hopped off and walked up the hill to her apartment. She walked past people but didn't really see them. She was in a trance. She reached her apartment, took off her shoes and walked up the steps. She opened the door, threw her bag on the table, took off her clothes, and walked around in her bra and panties. It was her apartment, and she could do whatever she wanted to.

She sat on the couch, looking across Florida Islands. It was so captivating from where she lived. It could have been wonderful to share this beautiful view in someone's arms with a glass of red wine, she thought, but tonight it was just her and a glass of water. After she finished drinking her water, she dropped on the floor like a dead person and fell fast asleep, without taking a shower. She was exhausted.

--------

She woke up in the middle of the night to the sound of thundering rain, dropping like hail on the roof, and the cold wind bristling on her delicate skin. It was cold and dark outside, and she could hardly see anything. She got up and closed all the windows. Then she took a shower. She made herself a cup of tea afterward. There was enough warmth in the house, but she was cold inside. There was no warmth under the sheets at night. It was lonely and frustrating. She needed to do something about it, rather than hoping for a miracle to happen. She knew she was equipped and armed to get the job done, but it had been annoying for a while. She sat on the balcony in the dark, sipping her cup of tea and sobbing. Her tears dropped in the cup, making it difficult to make a distinction between teardrops and tea. She wondered why life was so unfair. She had so many unanswered questions running through her head. Why couldn't a good woman with a decent and stable job not find a good man who met her standards and opinions?

She went to work every day, hoping to see Maduku again. During her tea breaks, she sat on the bench outside the hospital, eating sugarcane, bananas, and avocados, hoping to see Maduku walking through the corridor to the children's ward. She yearned to see him. Every morning, when she woke up, I was the very first thing on her mind. She was hypnotized and mesmerized by me in her waking moments. She was obsessed and emotionally crazy about me, yet all without me even knowing it. She was a secret admirer who adored me from a distance, and it was killing her inside.

At work, she would often peep through the window at her desk to see if Sister Martha and I might arrive in the corridor, walking toward the children's ward. She would often walk down the corridor toward the entrance, just to see if I might be standing outside chatting with the sick patients. As the chance of seeing me slowly faded away, she started doubting whether she was beautiful or not. And if she was beautiful, why was she not attracting anyone? Or did men not approach her for fear of rejection because she was a professional? She was battling these thoughts in her mind, and suicidal thoughts started to creep in. But she was determined to keep hope alive.

Weeks and months passed, but I didn't visit. She decided to take it upon herself to do something about it rather than leave it to chance. She decided to go to church, the place that she had neglected her entire life. She thought that Maduku might be attending church with the sisters. So she decided to go the next Sunday.

Sunday morning came, and the gorgeous nurse was on a quest to find me at a place she had never thought of checking before, the church. The church was situated on a hill with a captivating view overlooking the harbor. She put on something nice and applied a little perfume. Arriving in front of the church, she was cordially greeted by a gentleman. He was tall, dark, and handsome. His job was to usher people into the building. He led her to the second row from the front and invited her to sit. The building was packed to capacity, but people were still arriving. A word of welcome and prayer was given and offered to start the meeting.

After words of welcome and prayers were said, a young, vibrant, and energetic young man with black curly hair walked to the podium, grabbed a microphone and started the singing part of the service with fast songs. The harmony of the people's voices resounded. The atmosphere was electrifying. People were tapping their toes and snapping their fingers to the rhythm of blues. They found release from within while singing. The songs were like water that quenched and refreshed the soul. They brought comfort and healing to the soul. It was amazing what the power of a good song could do. The nurse thought it was like medicine.

After the fast songs, a few slow, soft, and soothing ones were introduced to the people. The music was soft and tender. The people were in awe of the music and in love with the lyrics of the songs. They got lost in the harmony and the melody. The words were like honey on their lips, so sweet and so satisfying to the spirit. The songs were like a surgeon's knife. They cut deep into the core of one's being and revealed the intents, contents, and secrets of the heart. Only the words of a song could perform such a difficult task. They cut deep into a person's' heart and soul, and have the amazing ability to travel to places where no human can go.

After the slow songs, it was time for the preaching of the word. The preacher delivered a very powerful message. He titled his message "The Beauty of Singleness." It was a message aimed for those who were planning to settle down with someone because they worried their biological clock was ticking. The preacher hoped his words would slow the unmarried down from rushing into responsibility and embrace their singleness in its entirety.

I am going to talk to you about the beauty of singleness, of not being married, and hopefully, at the end of my message, you will go home and give serious thought to rushing into living with responsibility. And if you are rushing around, you might want to slow down and allow life's circumstances to reveal the true colors of a potential partner. Then you can decide if you want to sleep with what you see for the rest of your life, until death. And if you are already married, you will see perhaps, for the first time, the beauty of singleness and its benefits, which some of you have been missing out on.

There were smiles of guilt, regret, and great anticipation in the building. The people in the church were greatly excited to hear about the "beauties" of singleness spelled out from the podium.

When you are single, you are free to go anywhere without anyone checking on you. You can stay up late watching your favorite game or movie without anyone bothering you to listen to their stressful day. You can spend an evening drinking tea till late at a friend's house without anyone looking for you. When you are single, you can spend your money on what you like without consulting anyone, because it's your money. When you are single, you can manage your own space. You control who can come in, and who may not. You can talk to your relatives, the female ones, and no one is asking who those females are you are talking to. You can go back to college and take a course to better yourself professionally. You can stay up all night reading and chew through the books, and sleep in without any hurry to make breakfast. You are answerable and accountable to no one about how you should live your life with respect to your time and resources.

You are literally in charge of your own life when you are single. It's a beautiful life. You can come home late after work, and no one's going to ask where you have been. You have no emotional obligation. But if you are independent and have it all together, then you are ready for marriage. You are ready for marriage when you don't need to think about it. If you spend a lot of time thinking about it, then you are not ready for marriage.

This is what I learned from my mentor, my late father, who was a priest. This is what he likened marriage to. Think of being single as a glass full of water, filled right to the brim. That's what it means to be single. You are so fulfilled and consumed in your singleness that there is no room for any distraction to creep in. And the person that you want to marry should be a full glass of water, too. Now when you two meet and decide to give of yourselves to each other, what happens? Overflow is the outcome. They give to each other not because they need to but because they decide to give. It's a decision not made because they want something or expect something in return. They give without expectation. It's a natural expression. Giving is natural, not manipulative or conditional.

Now if you spend time thinking and looking for a mate, then you are like a glass half full, and you are looking for someone to fill you up. And if you meet another half-full person, when they fill you up, they are empty and vice versa. That is why we have tensions and frictions in a lot of marriages today—two half-full people trying to live together and fill each other up. What we want to see is two full glasses of water endeavor to live together in a matrimonial and contractual covenant. We want to see overflowing that can affect society and the nation as a whole in a positive way. When we reach that stage, then we are mature. This is where giving to the significant other is a natural expression of one's maturity.

The nurse listened attentively to every single point the preacher made. She agreed with every one of them. She could see what she was going to miss if she was impatient and rushed into finding someone to live with.

Singleness is the most important state in a person's life. It gives you the opportunity to know yourself before you join with another. It is also a time for developing oneself professionally so as to be an asset to the person you give yourself to. You are giving something that has value and enhances the other. You are not a liability. If you develop yourself to be an asset during your single years, when the time comes for you to share your life with someone, you are literally going to give value to the other person.

That's one reason for remaining single. You use your time and resources to better yourself, to improve yourself, to add value to the person you are viewing as a potential spouse for life. Most people are ignorant about this very important concept. They spend their time running around, looking for a mate. They are like a leech, looking for someone to place their sucker on for emotional stability and convenience. These kinds of people are dangerous people. They are a liability and just want to take without giving.

This is one extra point for your notes, if you are taking any. Now it may sound a little bit objective, but you need to take this into consideration when choosing a soulmate, especially you ladies. Some birds, when they are ready to lay eggs, prepare the nest first. Some prepare a hole in a tree. Before she lays her eggs, she will first prepare a nest or a hole. If you are dating a guy, ask him if he has prepared a nest for you and your babies? This is very important! Ask him if he has prepared for you to give birth? If not, don't date him for heaven's sake. Don't just fall for a bloke because he's handsome or has a degree or a fancy car. If he doesn't own a house and is still living with his parents, he isn't prepared or ready to look after you, period.

When the nurse heard this very important point about developing and bettering oneself to be an asset and the prerequisite for dating a prospective husband, she was literally blown away. She was cut to the core of her being. It was an awesome concept. She had never heard of that before. Many of her religious affiliates never knew this either. They warmed the pews listening to shallow sermons with no substance or depth, pretty much like a grocery shopping list type of sermon. Most of those sermons were all emotion and motivation but lacked the ability to bring change and transformation to a person's life. She refocused her thoughts to listen as the preacher continued.

So many people who rush into marriage don't have the opportunity to better themselves, to be assets, to add value to another person's life. They squander their time and energy on worthless things. They spend their single years searching for what they think is the ideal mate, rather than preparing themselves to be the ideal mate. I encourage those who are still single, the unmarried ones, to start working on yourself to be an asset. You don't have much time to waste. Stop wasting time on friends who are going nowhere in life, aimless with no sense of direction. The next chapter of your life is marriage.

And marriage is like an omelet. It is just as good as the eggs in it. Bad eggs, bad omelet. Good eggs, good omelette. Work on your egg first before you crack another egg. You don't want to end up with a stinking omelette. I will talk more about that next time, that is totally different series. It would take probably a week or two for me to really talk about marriage. It's a topic where I will literally show you in practical terms how to work on your egg.

The preacher closed with a word of prayer, and the Sunday meeting was over. The nurse's expectation of meeting Maduku was met with disappointment, but she had a new insight into her purpose and destiny. She chatted with the preacher during refreshments. She thanked him for his powerful delivery on the beauty of singleness. The pearls of wisdom dispelled by him were priceless. She left the church that Sunday a different lady with renewed purpose and passion, and a clear sense of direction where she wanted to go in life.

She walked down the concrete steps, almost a hundred steps or so. She could see the boats berthing in the harbor. She believed there was someone out there for her. When the time was right, her prince would show up and sweep her off her feet. She decided to stay focused on her work and keep her hope alive. She went to work with optimism and dedication to the task she had set for herself. She decided to remain positive and open even if the chance of seeing Maduku again was slipping away. Remembering what the preacher had said, she began to commute to work on public transport to save money for a down payment on a house.

# Chapter 7

## In Honiara, at the Hospital

Monday morning, the start of a new week. This was the day that fate finally smiled and remembered Nurse Fefenu for all that she had been through. Her lonely nights would soon be over.

As she was heading to work on the bus, a young man five years younger than she came in and sat next to her. His boots were dirty and so were his work pants. There was dirt on his torn boots. He was a plumber. Noticing that he was uncomfortable sitting next to a lady in a nursing uniform, she assured him that she didn't mind his dirty work clothes being next to her. She asked him what he did for a living. He said he was a plumber.

"If you don't mind me asking, how much did you earn for what you are doing?" she said.

"It depends, to be honest. If it is a contract job, twenty to thirty grand in a few months."

"Are you serious? Wow! That's unreal. You earn more than government workers and most people working in the private sector. Most of them could not earn even close to what you are making in a month. You see them in suits and shiny boots, driving flashy and fancy cars and still paying back the bank. Some even borrow money from their boss or friends to keep the family afloat, waiting for the next paycheck. They are living in debt from paycheck to paycheck. They parade a good face in the public eye, but in private, they are struggling to find joy and happiness, and can't find it in the things they amass and possess," she said.

"I heard some of those stories. I feel for people and families like that. They are sad stories, really, to even think about. Some brothers end up leaving their wives and kids behind. They do not have the grit to handle the daily pressures and challenges of living. All they bank on to keep the family going is the job they are holding down, even if it offers little pay and less sleep. It puts food on the table. It's tough. Where I live, some people borrow money from me to pay for their kids' school fees or to put fuel into the car to drive to work or drop the kids off at school. I am doing pretty well because I am single. I don't have too many commitments and responsibilities. I am happy with my life right now. I am financially comfortable, which is a good thing," the young plumber said.

"You are still single? What is wrong with all the girls in your neighborhood?" the nurse gasped.

"I don't know. I reckon they probably don't like a dirty man fixing toilets and stinking of septic. But I am not desperate at all. I am happy being single. There is less stress and more freedom. You can do anything you want, go wherever you want without someone asking and checking on you."

"Well, it's nice meeting and talking with you. I work at the hospital, working with sick kids in the children's ward. Where do you work? in town?"

"I work for East West Plumbing on 82 Hibiscus Avenue. It's not hard to find me. We are situated near Ocean Breeze Shipping Services. I am out most of the time, attending jobs outside of the city. If I'm not available, leave a message with the receptionist. She is a lovely girl with good people skills. She is helpful and kind," he said as he left the bus.

The nurse got off at the hospital. She could not believe that the plumber was still single, already successful and making tons of money. She didn't understand if he was single by choice or if the girls were picky and too selective, setting their sights on someone with an MBA degree or a solicitor or an office clerk, jobs considered attractive by parents who want their daughters to marry someone with a college diploma or degree.

When she arrived at her desk, she looked through the register to see if any new patients had been admitted. She checked on her patients to ensure that they were taking their medications as instructed. After checking on her patients, she walked to the restroom and noticed water all over the floor. There was a leak in the cistern. It was a plumbing problem and needed to be fixed before the whole ward was flooded. She went to report the problem to her supervisor.

"There is a leak in the cistern in the toilet, and water is all over the floor. It needs to be fixed immediately before the whole children's ward gets flooded."

"Do you know someone or a plumbing company in town who can fix that problem?" he asked.

"Yes, I do. I know a guy who works for a company in town called East West Plumbing. He can fix that problem for us." Nurse Fefenu tried to keep her excitement hidden.

"Alright, we better go right now and ask for help before it gets worse." She jumped in the car with her supervisor.

They arrived at East West Plumbing just before the guy was heading off to attend a job outside of town. "Hello gorgeous, what's happening? Is everything alright?" the plumber asked.

"As soon I arrived at work, I went to the restroom, and the cistern was broken and the floor was covered with water. It needs fixing immediately before it gets worse. We can't afford to delay or wait any longer. To delay would be disastrous," Nurse Fefenu explained.

"Not a problem. Too easy. I am coming with you guys right now," he said.

"How do you know him?" her supervisor asked while the plumber went to the tool shed to get his tools.

Nurse Fefenu blushed. "I met him on the bus this morning. He came and sat next to me. We chatted on the bus on my way to work. I asked what he did for a living, and he told me he was a plumber. I was shocked to realize that he is still single. I asked what was wrong with all the girls in his neighborhood, and he said they were probably looking for a bloke with an MBA qualification or a clerk or lawyer or something. Plumbing guys are considered dirty and stinky because they fix toilets and sewage. Parents want their daughters to marry someone working in the office."

"Guess what," the supervisor said. "I am a college graduate, a professional working in the medical field. And what I earn in a fortnight is not enough to pay my bills and leave a little for recreation. I need to do something besides my regular job. The figure looks big on the payslip, but the deductions really chew away a huge portion of what I earn. I feel like I am a failure. I don't do enough to give my wife and kids a better shot in life. I pretend to be doing all right, but I am struggling in private, barely making it through. For ages, the hourly rate hasn't increased. What I am paid an hour does not equate to the time and effort that I put in. So many times I want to leave the job. I work not because of I want to, but because of necessity. Job stability is the one thing holding me back from leaving. Even if you don't put your heart and soul into it, you can still have your job though the pay is not attractive. And even if you don't put in your best, you still get paid for showing up every day. In the past, I have tried so many times to quit, but I can't leave because of the stability of the job. I go to work every day for the paycheck, whether I do a good job or not. The hospital is my place for making money." He suddenly looked very tired and sad.

"I am a professional too, like you, working in the same field as you. I have had moments when I wanted to quit nursing, but the commitment I made to myself and to the job of serving people is what keeps me going, no matter what. Serving people, especially sick children, is a rewarding experience for me. Seeing the smile on their faces on the road to normal health is just inspiring and uplifting. I love being a nurse. I love serving sick kids. I love hearing their big ideas and dreams. I love hearing what they want to achieve and become when they grow up. Kids are fascinating. They are constantly dreaming. They never stop. The only thing missing in the equation for me right now is that special someone. I feel that I am ready and at a point in my life where I know what is important as opposed to what is urgent. There are urgent things, but they are not important things. I know that important things have to do with priority. And I won't settle for urgent things. Marriage is important and a priority for me. I know that two is better than one. They complement and bring out the best in each other. I have some things in my heart where I need a committed and dedicated husband to materialize in the world," she said.

The plumber returned, and the three of them headed for the hospital. When they arrived, the plumber asked, "So where is the broken cistern?"

The supervisor and the nurse led the plumber to the restroom. There was water all over on the floor when they arrived.

"Are you married with kids?" the supervisor asked the plumber.

"No. I am still single," he replied as he checked for where the cistern was leaking.

"Why aren't you married?" the supervisor continued. "Do you remain single by choice or did you have a bad experience? Did someone break your heart? Or was the dowry payment too expensive?"

The plumber chuckled. "I don't know. Ladies probably don't like dirty and stinking people, people who fix toilets and sewage. Maybe I should go out socializing or start going to church on Sundays," he said to the supervisor.

"Yes, that's a good idea. You might find a good and holy one."

"I'm not sure about finding holy ones in church. How do you know they are holy? You might meet a wolf in sheep's clothing," Nurse Fefenu said, joining the conversation.

"Yeah, it's hard to tell a wolf from a sheep in church," the plumber said, laughing out loud. "Plumbing is generally viewed as a dirty job. The first thing that comes to people's minds when they hear plumbing is fixing toilets and sewage. But it is a lot more than just fixing toilets and sewage. It is a rewarding career. The money is attractive. What you earn in a month can sustain you for two to three months if you decide to go on a vacation, especially if you are single like me. I love my job. Fixing things brings me joy. Connecting water to a new house brings me joy. You can have what you want in a matter of months if you are licensed to do the job. What takes a decade or fifty years for some people to achieve in respect to their goals and dreams, you can nail it in just a year or two. I was surprised when I owned two homes just a year after graduating from technical school. I couldn't believe it. Now I am working on getting my third home, and I am still in my mid-twenties," the plumber said.

The nurse and the supervisor were shocked when the plumber mentioned that he owned two homes debt-free. The supervisor was still paying his mortgage, and the nurse was still renting. They thought their diplomas could attract more money, but the plumber proved them wrong. But they knew that their college certificates could give them the lifestyles they dream about if they were willing to put in the necessary work and discipline.

"I put my heart and soul into what I am doing," the plumber continued. "I don't do half-hearted jobs because your job is a reflection of you. What you do reveals the kind of person you are. You might appear charming and be perceived as a nice person, but what you do with your hands and time reveals even more, your attitude and the values you stand for."

The supervisor was cut to the core. A sense of guilt and shame entered his soul. He had been considering finding a job other than nursing. What the plumber said sounded like a rebuke to his lousy attitude.

The supervisor was thinking about asking the plumber if he could work with him as an apprentice to gain some experience. He wanted to shift from nursing to plumbing. He thought the fastest way to gain experience in plumbing was to work with the plumber instead of spending four years at a technical institute. He also figured out that a certificate in plumbing doesn't do the work. It's people who eventually do the work. So experience is more important than a piece of paper. A reference from the plumber would do if he wanted to go solo in the future.

"All right, it's fixed now. East West Plumbing will send the bill through the post," the plumber said. "It's a pleasure meeting you. If we encounter similar problems in the future, you know the guy and company to call."

They dropped him off at East West Plumbing. "I will call in someday to see you. I want to talk to you about something," the supervisor said.

"No worries, mate. Now you know where I work." As soon as they dropped him off, he hopped on his truck to do a job outside of town. He was a busy man, vibrant and energetic. He was always smiling and didn't talk too much. The East West Plumbing clients loved him for his dedication and commitment to the task at hand.

On their way back to the hospital, the supervisor looked at Nurse Fefenu and smiled.

"What is the smile about?" she asked.

"I smile because the plumber could be a potential partner for you. He is already financially stable and has two homes, and is working on acquiring his third. You could be an ideal wife for him. He is a very good worker and is passionate about his work. What more could you ask for in a man? And you as a nurse have a compassionate, nurturing, and caring heart. You two would make a powerful combination as a couple to impact the world. I could see the compatibility between you two. If I was you, I would definitely give it a shot and see how it goes. I can tell that he likes you, but he was just too shy to make it show. You have nothing to lose," the supervisor said.

The nurse was laughing out loud, hitting her left thigh with her left hand. "I'm serious. Go home after work and think about it. I am daring and encouraging you to give it a shot. You never know what's around the corner," he said laughing, as they turned into the entrance of the hospital.

The nurse reckoned it was a good idea.

After work, the nurse went home. She sat down on the couch in her apartment all by herself, sipping a cup of tea after a nice warm shower, ruminating on the words her supervisor had said regarding the plumber. She thought that her supervisor was dead right, and when she put the plumber and Maduku on a pendulum of financial stability, it tended to be weighing more heavily on the plumber's side.

After a careful examination of what they could offer and bring to the table, the plumber had a lot on his plate already. Comparing them with respect to what they did for a living, Maduku was not even close, not one inch, to what the plumber had achieved and continued to achieve. Maduku still had a long way to go to be financially secure and stable because financial stability was vitally important to her. He still had many options to choose from. He was green and still wanted to explore and discover the world out there in its glory and splendor. He probably wasn't sure which route to take after he graduated from college, and something might change during his time at college. And if landed a job in the field he was going to study, she was nervous if he would be able to sustain her financially. Maduku was not ready financially or emotionally to settle down, she felt. A woman needed to be financially stable and secure, and a man could do that for her.

With the plumber, she could have the peace of mind of living in her own home. The plumber was like a bird who prepared a nest for her to lay her eggs inside. She could be financially secure and stable, and not worry about how she would pay the mortgage and the doctor's bills, or how she would feed her kids and tuck them into bed at night knowing that they were safe from harm or fear, or how she could pay for their college education. With the plumber, she could quit her job if she wanted to and be a housewife, nurturing dend applying discipline to her kids, teaching them how to live and earn respect in the community. She could achieve a lot more with the plumber than she could with Maduku. She and the plumber could seize the opportunity and claim the future together. They could design and own the future, using their talents and abilities.

Her careful analysis of Maduku and the plumber had come to an end. She made up her mind and chose the plumber over Maduku. It was her choice, and she was willing to sleep with that choice until her dying day.

Reaching that serious conclusion required some action to be taken, and she needed to be proactive about it. To back up her thoughts with deeds, she needed to write a letter to the plumber, expressing her feelings and desires to be his wife, future partner, and best friend. She eventually ended up writing the letter and posted it to East West Plumbing with the plumber's name clearly written on the envelope.

To her surprise, the plumber replied and said yes to her application. They got married and left the hospital and the city to work in one of the islands in the eastern part of the country. With the cooperation of the community that they moved into, they created a model village called the "Power of One."

That model has been duplicated many times over in villages near and far. The couple loves the community spirit exhibited by the people. The Power of One model has revived and reignited the communal spirit that had fizzled out due to long-standing greed and personal ambition. The beauty of owning their own homes felt good and reassured them that they could achieve more if they maintained the community flame burning with trust and integrity in them.

People pitched in to help, the sweat equity was the choir force of progress behind the model. Everybody had a decent roof over their heads. The next challenge was how to generate wealth without leaving home and going to distant shores in search of opportunity and work. The plumber and his wife decided to travel overseas, and Ms. Fefenu helped her husband assure the people that they would have some ideas to implement when they returned.(Yes, instead of Ms. Fefenu, put Mrs Susuburi, her husband's surname)

They were the proud parents of twins who were born abroad while they were traveling. They were able to choose between working for money and traveling the world. They acquired even more houses after having their first children. They traveled for three months every year. The nurse was so thrilled that she had waited and not rushed into finding an adorable husband, the man of her dreams. Her patience finally paid off. She had initially asked for financial security and stability, but life had been very generous and given her adventure as well.

# Chapter 8

# At the Sisters Residence, Honiara

Meanwhile, my travel arrangements to study at the college had been finalized. I was granted a study visa for three years. My return ticket had been paid, and I was due to fly on the next Saturday. The two sisters, Martha and Mary, decided to host a small evening tea for me. They invited their close-knit family to come and share the evening with us. Also, religious friends and former high school classmates who were now teachers and nurses at various clinics and schools in the city came, and a retired electrical engineer was also one of the invited people. Unfortunately, Brother Andrew Suumalefo was away on a mission to the West Coast, but I had met him for lunch at the sisters' house. So, although he was missed, it was not a big deal.

There was local food in abundance, organically grown on the plains of Guadalcanal. The richness of the plains washed down from the mountains and found its resting place in the plains. The locally grown food was free of pesticides and chemicals. While we were eating, Sister Mary got up from her chair and uttered a few remarks of gratitude to the people for coming. She briefly touched on how she and Martha had met me through the good work they had done in my village. She talked about how the work had died from greed and irresponsibility.

After she spoke, Sister Martha got up and reaffirmed what Sister Mary had said. She had been ecstatic to meet a young man from the area that they had been working in who had won a scholarship to study abroad. Although the good work had fallen apart, life had a way of preserving a seed of hope to emerge where it seemed like there was no hope.

"We hope to see Maduku in a place of responsibility and service after he graduates. There is so much untapped potential in the area he comes from, and it needs a visionary to maximize the potential and convert the available resources into cash.And that visionary could well be Mr. Maduku Mamata" Martha said. Their friends and family gave her a round of applause as she returned to her seat.

Now it was my turn to say thank you to the sisters' and the people who had gathered.

"I would like to express my sincere and deepest gratitude to Sisters Mary and Martha for the wonderful hospitality they have given me. You are wonderful and extraordinary hosts. Thank you so much for the support you have given me. I will never forget it as long as I live. I will cherish the memories for the rest of my life. The spirit of love and grace you have exhibited in everything you do is exceptional. It manifests in your home and outside of the home, and in everything your hand touches, including the food you cook in the kitchen. It is true that what a woman does is a reflection of her heart and her state of happiness. It's not that hard to tell when a woman is happy and when she is not. You can see it through the work of her hands. So I am learning a little bit more about women during my short stay in your home," I said.

With a respectful nod to the sisters, I continued. "And to the friends of Sisters Mary and Martha, thank you very much for coming. Your presence this evening means a lot to me, even though I may not know you personally. Your acquaintance, friendship, and connection to these two sisters speak volumes. You made this evening possible. You made this evening a reality, and I am honored and humbled tonight to share in food and in friendship with you. I am not the likeliest candidate to be granted this scholarship to study Human Resource Management at a prestigious institute abroad, but I am grateful and blessed beyond measure for the opportunity given to me, not out of personal merit but purely due to my healthy grades. I worked very hard and experienced many sleepless nights of study during high school. I had to earn this scholarship through hard work and countless hours of studying and reading. From what I have been told, I'm probably the only candidate from my area to get a scholarship in a very long time. Perhaps there has never been a person from my region to receive a prestigious award for further study in college.

"I believe it is crucial for people to be trained to be productive," I said. "My area is underdeveloped and static in terms of industrial development and has been that way for well over three decades now. We don't have the mechanism or technology to better manage the natural resources we have. Getting this scholarship is the opportunity and the only chance my people and I seek to pull the region forward in development. I would like to close by saying thanks. Thank you so much for the support you have shown in coming this evening.

The friends and family of the sisters gave me a round of applause for my brief and concise remarks. Shortly after I had finished talking, a retired electrical engineer walked over to me and shook my hands.

"Congratulations! That was impressive! I am Zebedee Akoako, an electrical engineer, although I retired a few years ago. I met Sisters Mary and Martha many years ago when they used to fly overseas doing mission work. I am happily married to a beautiful woman of Scottish descent. We have three kids who are living with my wife's parents overseas. They come to visit on holidays, but they want to come back and work here in the islands after they graduate. They have a passion for serving people and want to work with in our communities. I took them to my village when they were little. They had a wonderful experience and fond memories of the people and the lifestyle. They were blown away when they saw the smiles and happiness on the people's faces, even though they didn't have much money or many material possessions. Eating lobsters, snappers, and mud crab for free in the village was what got them hooked on wanting to serve in the community."

"Wow, that is inspiring!" I said. "Your kids embody the spirit of community and service. They want to serve people with their gifts and talents. They probably found something bigger than their own private ambitions and want to make a difference in people's lives. That's exactly my motivation for living, too. The very reason for my existence is to serve people with my gifts and talents without expecting anything in return. I had that purpose written down on paper. I was so clear about what I wanted to do in life. There is no guessing about it."

"You sound exactly like my kids, young man," he continued. "Your passion for serving people without reciprocation is amazing. You are one of a kind. It's hard to find people with a philosophy like that—serving without expecting anything in return. It's like an apple tree that never complains when people pick its fruit and leave without saying thanks. It doesn't hurt its feelings. The tree just keeps on serving by bringing forth more fruit the next season. The world would be a little better if this kind of spirit inhabited us all, serving without expectation.

"I spent most of my time working at the airport. I loved my job and was fascinated by airplanes. It is mind-blowing to see massive equipment defy gravity for a small span of time. There is a principle involved in that transaction. To defy gravity, you need to activate another law. That is what airplanes do. They use the law of aerodynamics which causes the plane to lift. Aerodynamics operates on the principle of fuel. I won't go into the detailed computation of that transaction, but just to give you an idea, everything whether living or nonliving operates on a certain principle in life to achieve the desired outcome.

"One thing I discovered about airplanes is that they are expensive to maintain because only birds were meant to fly in the sky. It is cheaper for them. They don't need to be checked for mechanical or electrical faults before and after flying. Through that observation, I learned something right away: imitation is a costly exercise. When we imitate and want to be something that we are not meant or designed to be, it is costly. It costs us everything. It costs us our time and resources. We might pretend to be flying high and far beyond the blue, but we are doing it at a steep cost. Why? Because it is not natural. It is not inherent or inbuilt. When we discover our true selves, what we are meant to be, we can fly high with ease like the birds of the air. We will never complain or stress about flying for it is a joy to fly. If we complain about what we are doing in life, then apparently, we haven't discovered what we were born to do yet."

"That is a very important point, a powerful statement," I said. "Imitation is a costly thing. Most people are still grappling with discovering themselves, who and what they are, and what they are capable of doing. So they take on other people's personalities by cutting their hair funny or wearing a certain outfit to have some sense of value and importance. They attach themselves to things and people to get an identity. And when things and people change, their identity is gone. It will get worse in the years ahead. People will do a lot of crazy things to get an identity and attention. When we discover ourselves, we don't need to advertise to get attention. We just become like the apple tree you mentioned, bringing forth fruits without expecting anything in return. Birds are attracted or drawn to our tree because of the fruits we bear. If we are not attracting birds, then it simply means we are barren and unproductive.

"Yes," the retired engineer agreed, "people will lose their dignity and go insane to find meaning and significance in temporal things. They're disillusioned and unfulfilled, searching for meaning in artificial things. Anyway, nice to meet you, young man. Best of luck in your studies. I hope to see you somewhere in town or in a position of responsibility when you come home after college."

After tea, everybody left the sisters' home. They went back to their homes, extremely full and satisfied.

# Chapter 9

# Henderson Airport, Honiara

The time had finally come for me to leave for college. I was at the airport checking in along with passengers traveling to destinations all over the world. The airport was full. Some of the passengers were loggers, going back home to see their real wives. They were thousands and thousands of miles away from home and were lonely in the tropics. They often sought warmth, comfort, and company in the arms of women by giving them cash or treating them to a night at the resorts. Marital vows had no place in their books when they were away from home. In their minds, their marriages had never existed, and so it bore little meaning for them. It was common and normal for them to cross the line. They had sown mortal seeds in many beautiful wombs, and the products of these unions, although born out of wedlock, had grown up to be responsible and active participants in the economy, mostly in the trades sector and the sciences.

Next to me, a religious man was checking in for his trip. He was being sent to preach to a church in the country where I was going to study. He was excited and could not wait to deliver his message. Among this amazing group of passengers, pursuing different paths in life, were two vibrant and athletic young women who were bound to represent their country at the Olympics. They were in their early twenties, and their joy of seeing the world and competing alongside their fellow athletes from various countries was indescribable. They were so excited and proud to show their athleticism and make their country proud. They said they wanted to be an inspiration to other young women who aspired to excel not only in the world of sports but in any area they felt passionate about.

I bumped into an old man while I was checking in. He was flying to Fiji to witness the wedding of his daughter. He had had this girl in out of wedlock when he was on a short holiday with his boss. He didn't see her for years, yet his daughter had forgiven him for his neglect and irresponsibility as a father, and his lack of support to provide for her from birth to adulthood. His daughter had reached a point in her life where she needed her father to give her away into the hands and care of her new father, her future husband. This new man in her life would hopefully provide what she had been missing out on, the responsibilities of a father to provide, support, cultivate, nurture, counsel, comfort and protect that which came from his loins. It was a major responsibility that required serious consideration. Her father had tried to reach out to her many times in the past, but her mother objected. She eventually reached out to her father after her mother had died of chronic bronchitis. She forgave her father, knowing that he had tried.

I took my boarding pass from a beautiful young woman with dark skin and headed to the Solomon Airlines plane that was parked and waiting. As I entered the door, I saw these words on the wall, "Welcome on board. Thank you for flying with Solomon Airlines." I took my place in seat 22. Before take off, I could see people standing against the fence, waiting to see the massive aircraft take off from earth. It was a fascinating thing for them to see a massive object soar into the heavens from a place with no paved roads or signs to follow to their destinations.

The passengers on the flight fastened their seat belts. The plane's engine started, and the pilot introduced his cabin crew for the duration of the flight, three girls and a gentleman. I saw the engineers checking the plane before take off, making sure everything was working. The plane's engine began to roar, and it turned toward the runway. Finally, it left the earth and soared into the sky like a bird. We were cruising at altitude forty-five minutes after take off. For the first time, I experienced the principle of aerodynamics in action. I remembered the retired electronic engineer's brief mention of the law of aerodynamics and how it uses the principle of fuel.

I was amazed and in awe of the wonders that science had brought about. I could not fully comprehend what I was experiencing and couldn't fully wrap my mind around it.

While I was thinking about the amazing work that science has done, a gorgeous woman who was a flight attendant kindly asked if I wanted something to eat from the menu. The cost of the meal was included in my ticket. She had long brown hair and brown eyes. Her legs were so enthralling to look at. Her caramel skin, and smooth texture of her face and legs, smeared with coconut oil, were irresistible to me. Her waist curved like a guitar. Her presence commanded my attention. It was hard to ignore her when she walked down the aisle. "Here is the menu list. Look through to see what you want. Your ticket covers the bill, so don't worry. Go ahead and choose what you want," she said.

I hardly recognized any items on the menu. I was familiar with cassava, taro, and banana cooked with coconut milk. Then I saw sandwich on the list that seemed familiar. The beautiful flight attendant returned and asked me if I had made up my mind. "Have you decided on something to eat yet?" she asked.

"Just a sandwich and a can of coke, please," I said.

"Not a problem. I'll get that for you in a minute. It won't be long," she said.

She went to the café bar, bringing back the sandwich and the can of coke. "You want something hot to drink, like tea? I can make it for you if you want," she said.

"Just tea, please, and two spoons of sugar. Thank you," I replied.

"You are welcome." She was caring and thoughtful. The service on the flight was one of warmth and affection. She came back with the cup of tea and a piece of paper. "Here is my address, and I would love to keep in touch. I don't have an address back at home. It's quite expensive to have a post office box unless you run a business. I fly into the country three times a week, so I could easily receive letters through this address. I find you fascinating. There is something about you that catches my attention. Please write soon when you have time. By the way, my name is Ms. Kristina Salili. Nice meeting you, and all the best in your studies," she said and walked away.

As she walked toward the back of the plane, she turned and winked at me, but I couldn't work out what she was thinking. I put the piece of paper in my pocket as the plane began its descent.

"We are landing in thirty minutes. The temperature is twenty-five degrees celsius, 77 degrees fahrenheit, at the moment. If you are visiting, enjoy your stay. If you are a resident, welcome home," the pilot said. It seemed that some of the passengers were anxious, anticipating a hard landing, but the plane landed safely. The passengers left the aircraft and walked through to immigration and customs.

# Chapter 10

# St Andrew's College, Brisbane

I presented my passport to immigration and passed through customs with nothing to declare. I found myself in the arrival lounge, standing with a group of people. I saw a tall man with glasses walking around with a cardboard sheet in his hands with my name written on it. When I saw this, I raised my right hand.

"You must be Maduku, right?"

"Yes, sir," I replied cheerfully.

"Nice to meet you. I'm Simon. Welcome to our beloved country. Australia."

Simon took out a two-dollar gold coin and deposited it into a payphone. He was calling his wife. "Hey sweetheart, Maduku and I are waiting for you at the pickup bay."

"No worries, I'm coming. I'll be there in five minutes." I could hear her through the receiver.

"My wife parked outside to avoid the parking fees. They are crazy!"

Simon said. While we were waiting for Simon's wife to arrive, I mistook Kristina's address for a cash receipt from a tee shirt that I had bought back on the island, and I threw it in the trash bin nearby. Simon's wife arrived, and we jumped in the car.

"This is my beautiful wife Jessica. She is my world and my everything. She made me into the man I am today. I would never have gotten to where I am without her. She is just amazing, and I am so blessed to have her in my life as a wife, partner, and best friend. She has given me two beautiful kids, a boy, and a girl, both who have left home already. My daughter is married, and my son is still studying at University," Simon said.

"Hi Maduku, how was your flight?" Jessica asked while turning at the intersection that led to the highway into the city.

"Pretty good," I replied. "It is my first time to fly in an airplane."

"Was the plane full?"

"Yes, it was. I was being looked after by a kind, thoughtful, and caring flight attendant," he said.

"That's nice to hear," Jessica said.

"She actually wants to keep in touch."

"Really? That's interesting. Is she Caucasian or Pacific Islander?" Simon asked.

"Pacific Islander, from my country. She comes from an island known for dancing all night to the island vibes and reggae beat. On the weekends, they dance until the sun comes up in the morning. The island has produced some fine dancers, men and women, and the most beautiful girls in the country come from that island. If you marry a girl from that island, and her family and people like you, they will cook soup and give it to you to eat. After you eat the soup, you will forget about your people and where you come from. That soup is cooked with some ginger and other herbs that are preserved in a sacred place, accessible only by the chief," I explained.

"I'm intrigued. I would love to visit that island one day and taste that kind of soup," Simon said laughing.

Jessica looked at Simon and kept driving. "In this country, you rarely get that sort of easy connection, unless you meet her at the pub or you both attend the same church. For a lady to give you her contact details before she even really knows you well must mean you are entertaining and fun and make her laugh uncontrollably or something. It's possible you are smooth, entertaining and appear friendly, offering to take her to the cinema to watch a blockbuster that just came out from Hollywood. When she gives you her phone number, she gives you access to her world. She is literally giving you the master key. It takes skill to make that happen. It's a good skill for you to master, especially if you are young and still looking around," Jessica said with a smirk.

"You have siblings?" Simon asked, changing the subject.

"No, it's only me. My parents passed away when I was two."

"Oh, I'm sorry," Jessica said.

" After my parents passed, I was raised by my aunt," I explained.

"What does she do?"

"She is a subsistence farmer. She works and plows the land, growing vegetables and other root crops like potatoes, cassava, yams, and taro. She grows a bit of everything you can eat. She is a great woman, very generous. She has a big heart, although she doesn't tolerate laziness and idleness. One day, many years ago, her husband went fishing and never came home. He disappeared like smoke and vanished like a breeze, never to be seen again. A search was conducted, but had to be called off due to bad weather. It was a tragic time for her family."

There was silence in the car for about twenty minutes before Simon spoke. "You have been through so much. To emerge from that unimaginable chapter strong and more determined is inspirational. I believe this scholarship is a tremendous opportunity for you to save your family and your people. In my opinion, since listening to your story and your background, you are like Joseph in Egypt in the Bible, that old testament tale. You come out here so you can learn and gather information. You cannot help your family and your people if you are not equipped to help them out of the situation they are in.

My wife and I will try to give you our best in hosting you for the first six months until we can find an apartment for you to move into. We want you to have a good experience and a memorable stay with us before you move to live on your own. Consider your time with us as an orientation. We will teach you the culture of the place, so you don't need to assimilate. We would rather have you adapt. Basically it's just about how to use what's in the house, like the washing machine, toaster, stove and so forth, and how to maneuver through the city, traveling on public transport, the buses, trains, and ferries, and how to show courtesy to the people in the community and in everyday life. Tomorrow, we will take you around town for a bit of sightseeing and to see your new school. Sound good?"

"Absolutely."

We arrived at Simon and Jessica's place. The first thing Jessica showed me was the bathroom and toilet. She cooked broccoli with chicken, onion, curry, and garlic for tea. It was so delicious, I went back for seconds. After tea, I took a shower like I had at Sister Martha and Mary's place, balancing the hot and cold water. Jessica showed me how to use the hot and cold water system, and I explained that I had learned how to use it when I lodged with Sister Martha and Mary.

I watched a movie with Simon and his wife. They told me to feel at home and not to be shy. If I needed help with anything, I was just to ask. I slept under a comforter because it was quite cool, being that it was winter in Australia. I had never slept under a warm blanket back in the village. There, I slept on a mat, sewn and knitted from coconut fronds, with no protection from mosquitos or roaches. For most of my life, I had listened to mosquitos singing to me at night.( I replace home umbrella with just mat, woven out of coconut fronds)

Sleeping on a mattress under a comforter was cozy and warm. There were no more mosquitoes singing in my ears. I was adapting very quickly. Actually, I had already adapted before I arrived in Australia. It doesn't take me long to adapt to a new environment. I learn quickly, and am hungry and willing to learn something new every day.

The next morning, I woke up and had bacon, eggs, and toast for breakfast. It was good to have something different for a change. In the village, I had never tasted bacon and eggs on toast. Bacon was either cooked in a bamboo or boiled in a pot, and the same applied to eggs. Having them simultaneously on toast was lovely and less work. That first morning, I started to fall in love with bacon and eggs on toast.

"Today, we will check in at your new school, but I'm not driving today," Jessica said.

"We will catch the bus to the city, and then catch the train to the campus. We will also check in at the museum and the state library. If we have time, we might jump on the ferry along Brisbane river. That's the plan for the day," explained Simon.

Jessica gave me a pair of Adidas boots that she had bought at a garage sale. It was chilly so she gave me a black leather jacket, black denim jeans, and a black cap. I was dressed in black, head to toe. I realized I love everything black when it comes to clothing. Jessica made sure that I stayed warm and comfortable. We walked to the bus station and caught the bus to the city. The bus was full. We arrived in the city and caught the train. People were rushing and moving fast, not smiling or talking to anyone, especially a stranger on the street. They were minding their own business. They were headed to who knows where, a different world than the one I knew. In my world, you smiled to anybody and everybody on the streets.

We hopped off the train at the campus. I noticed that some streets were named after people, like Elizabeth Street and George Street. The skyscrapers looked frightening, and they made me think of earthquakes and cyclones, especially Cyclone Namu in 1986, which crippled the economy of my country.

I liked my new school. I felt that this was the place, the environment, where I would find the solutions for the two problems that had become the purpose of my life. Here I would discover how to solve the two problems that had plagued my country for so long. After checking in at my new school, we caught the bus to the jetty and then the ferry, still using the same ticket we had been using all day. It was a daily ticket and could be used on all public transport in the city. We cruised along the Brisbane River. The river was clear of cans and plastics, but you could hardly see the fish or stones at the bottom, unlike the rivers back home.

We got off the ferry after cruising at South Bank. We walked past the pools, but in winter, not many people were swimming. "In summer, these pools will be jam packed with children and their parents. They have swimming instructors and supervisors around in case someone drowns or something. We might come here for a swim during the summer," Jessica said. "Can you swim?"

"Swimming is natural to us in the islands. We started swimming when we are little, around the age of five. And we don't need to take swimming lessons. Swimming in the river is a normal activity. I can swim across the Brisbane River to the other side without wearing a life jacket," I said. Jessica and Simon raised their eyebrows. "Can you really?" they asked.

"Sure," I said. "I capsized at sea one time and had to swim to shore without a life jacket. During massive floods, I swim across the river to collect bananas and coconuts that wash down from people's gardens along the river, and I can push a log that is floating downstream to the river banks so that I can have firewood. I don't know what the Brisbane River is like, but I could really swim across if there are no crocodiles," I said.

We arrived at the museum. Records, collections, and artwork by renowned artists and sculptors were displayed and stored at the museum. The staff was amazing. They had excellent people skills. They were exceptional at their jobs. They didn't remain silent and stare at people when they came in like the shops back home in Chinatown, where shop assistants would just stand behind the counter, staring and not smiling. They would often get mad when someone asked about the contents or details of a product. Customer service was poor because all they cared about was their paycheck. At the museum, it was different. They loved to answer questions. They were knowledgeable about their work. The way they dressed and presented themselves said it all about who they were and the kind of service they offered. It made the environment vibrant for everybody.

The day's sightseeing had come to an end, and it was time for us to go home. I was ecstatic. I couldn't wait to attend my first lecture of the semester. We took the same route home that we had taken to come into town. I was blown away by the tidiness and the evenness of the streets in the city. The streets were even and numbered. The footpath was paved. I saw firsthand the power of proper planning and implementation. I was impressed with how the taxpayers money was well spent because they deserve better services and infrastructure for their contributions.

We arrived home tired. Jessica did not feel like cooking tea. So Simon ordered takeout so she wouldn't have to cook. We had Kentucky Fried Chicken for tea. Even though it was my first time trying it, fried chicken became my favorite. I'm not fussy and will eat whatever is available. There was certainly no Kentucky Fried Chicken back home. Not even in Chinatown. What they had in Chinatown was fish and chips, often prepared and cooked in unhygienic environments. The restaurateurs only cared about money, not the customers' health. Health inspectors were often bribed to pass a restaurant, even if it failed to meet Food and Hygiene requirements and Occupational Health and Safety procedures. Health inspectors might have thought that they were compromising the health of strangers, but really, they were compromising the very health and well-being of their very own people.

# Chapter 11

# St Andrew's College

The academic semester had begun. The professor came in and introduced himself and the course of study for the semester. He spent about fifteen minutes in the class. He then told us to read the first four chapters of our textbook and he'd see us at the next lecture. I didn't understand. In high school, the teacher stayed with the students.

"Excuse me, professor, where are you going? You spent only fifteen minutes in the class and now you're leaving?" I asked.

"Yes, this is university now. You are no longer in high school. You need to start getting used to it. I am just a resource. Go home and do your readings, and write a report," the professor said.

I realized that my sponsors had paid thousands of dollars to an institution to tell me to go read a book at the library and write a book report. I was shocked. It was unreal. I was tempted to pack up and go home, but I stayed. I wanted to see the whole picture unfold, until the end. I remembered what Ms. Julia Adams, the receptionist at the embassy, had told me about her college experience. It was absolutely true what she had prophesied. College was about reading books about other people's ideas, and I would get certified after I had gained a certain number of ideas.

After living with the Simons for six months, I moved out and lived on my own in an apartment in Cleveland. I was now confident that I could commute to school on public transport and travel around town unassisted. My time with the Simons had helped me adapt to the culture and the lifestyle. They instilled confidence in me so that I could be independent and responsible to look after myself.

In my class, there was a gorgeous lady named Ms. Sarah Nanagalio. Her skin was the color of caramel candy, and she had big brown eyes. She was over six feet tall and had a charming personality and infectious smile. She had a tiger tattooed below her right shoulder. She had big earrings on her ears that made her look dignified. Her positive energy was contagious. When I met her for the first time, it felt like I had known her for ages. She seemed to glide as she walked. She commanded the attention of those in her presence. She had long sleek legs that were so captivating to look at. She sat next to me in the lecture sessions. She and a young man from the same country had both been granted a scholarship to my University. I could tell that her fellow countryman had feelings for her but was too shy to express them for fear of rejection and shame. I believe he had felt this way since primary school. With the passage of time, they had gone their separate ways in their high school journeys.

The male students in the class were too shy to approach her for a chat. Having the same skin color as Sarah gave me an advantage over my peers, and I decided to have a chat with her. I already possessed some skills. I could speak well, sing and play the guitar, drums, and the bass. I was self-taught, but I knew my most powerful strength was my ability to communicate well. My friends at school often refer to me as "sweet-talker" or "smooth man." I had the words and the stories to tell, and I was fun and entertaining to be around. Of course, this strength often got me into trouble, especially with the girls, because I learned that they love a man who can talk and take them on a mental journey through storytelling, a man who knows the beginning and the end of a story. I certainly had that ability of storytelling. I could transform a boring conversation into a lively, juicy, and entertaining tale.

Sarah's strength was mathematics. She was exceptionally fluent with numbers and complex equations. Her computation ability was immaculate and incredible. My strength was in words. I loved to read and learn about new words and their meanings. Sarah and I complemented each other in our respective strengths as students who were taking the same course – Human Resource Management.

As the academic semester progressed, I noticed Sarah carried a Bible, a pocket size one. She loved the Word and to meditate on scripture. Memorizing scripture was one of her favorite pastimes. I, like Sarah, loved the Word. Memorizing scripture was food for my soul. Sarah and I had a common interest. We both loved the word. This common interest gave me something to talk about with Sarah, anytime and anywhere on the campus. One day we took our common interest a step further, and we started competing to see who could memorize more scripture than the other. Girls love competing. Sarah eventually memorized more scripture than me, but I didn't care that Sarah had beaten me in scripture memorization.

I treasured our friendship more than anything, even more than memorizing scripture. Instead of going out on the weekends, we would spend time at the library, reading and memorizing scripture. Knowing so much scripture by memory might not have contributed very much toward our academic performance, but we got very good marks in our course assessments anyway. So we stuck with reading our books and memorizing scripture. It kept our minds healthy, and it contributed to our course of study, at least in my opinion.

From Cleveland, I commuted to school on the train. I was doing well in my readings and book reports. I was required to write a 2000-word essay on Human Resource Management, my core discipline of study. I had no difficulty at all tackling the topic because the title already told me what to write and what information to research. I not only knew what to write, but the number of paragraphs I had to write were already compressed in the title. The author's mind was hidden in the title. So in order to understand the author's mind, I simply looked at the words that made up the title. The title already told me what to write. So my job was to unwrap the author's mind in the words that made up the title.

Even though her strength was mathematics, Sarah helped me to read through my work, checking for spelling errors and any ambiguity in the use of technical jargon and language. Sarah wanted to pursue economics as her major. Reading and checking through my work confirmed that I had made good use of my strong vocabulary skills. Over the years, my mastery of words had grown very strong. I had a great variety of words to use to make my writing more engaging, entertaining, and fun to read while keeping the academic requirement of the assignment in sight and not straying from the theme and the message as I was contributing to a body of knowledge.

Winter came, and it was chilly and freezing, especially in the mornings. Sarah and I had been getting along very well, and we were very close. We became good friends. There were no more walls and fences. We would share lunch and talk about our hopes and dreams for the future and the countries that we each represented and loved. We were like a couple on the campus, inseparable. Our closeness allowed us to share the intimate secrets in our hearts. I was like Sarah's partner in crime.

One afternoon after class, Sarah asked me if he had a hobby or talent that I could share with her.

"Hey, Maduku," she said. "I'm just wondering if you have any hobbies besides scripture memorization, something that is a real talent?"

"Of course I have. I taught myself to play the guitar, bass, and drums, and I can sing a little bit, too. I learned by listening and observing. When someone would use a particular instrument, say a guitar or a bass, and put it down after playing it, I would pick it up and try to find my way around playing it. That's basically how I learned. I probably need to take music lessons."

"I want to hear you play and sing a song for me, an original," Sarah said.

"Not a problem at all."

"What about this Saturday? Come to the park. We'll meet there," she said.

"Sounds great!" I replied.

Sarah did not tell her fellow countryman, Mr. Timothy Kwairaga who had a crush on her in their primary school days, that she was going to meet me at the park. Sarah considered their friendship a platonic one, but Timothy wanted more than that. He had something else in mind, but was too nervous to express it to Sarah for fear of rejection and shame. They had parted ways when they transitioned to different high schools in their country. Sarah didn't tell Timothy about the upcoming meeting with me at the park. She kept it to herself and didn't want to invoke jealousy or put me in jeopardy. She was concerned that Timothy might get furious and want to fight me.

That Thursday evening, I went to Simon and Jessica's place for tea. After tea, I asked Simon if I could borrow his acoustic guitar to play a song for my classmate.

"Simon, I want to ask you about something," I said. "I have this friend from the Caribbean islands; Her name is Sarah, and she has beautiful caramel-colored skin. She is in my Human Resource Management class, too, but she wants to major in economics later on. She is exceptional in math. Her computation ability is mind-boggling. We became good friends. She asked me about my hobbies, and I said I could play the guitar, a bit of bass and drums. She was impressed and wanted to hear me play an original song for her at the park on Saturday."

"That's awesome! No worries. I can lend you my guitar. Sharing your talent with someone is a blessing in its own right. I didn't know that you are musical and could play a number of different instruments. You've got hidden talents, buddy. We encourage you to make the most of every opportunity that comes your way by connecting with people who are different from you through your music and talents. You know, don't despise the days of your humble beginnings. You never know which path those connections may lead to. And also, you never know what people might be going through in private. Sharing your music with them might help them get through whatever circumstances they are grappling with. Of course, you can take the guitar with you."

I attended a lecture on Friday and told Sarah that Simon and Jessica said I could meet her at the park. I told her that Simon had lent me his guitar. Sarah could not hold back her excitement. She jumped up and down and hugged me tight, kissing me on the cheek, which was a bit awkward for me. After class, we went to the library to ask for a book that was in the reserve collection. Sarah was the one who wanted to have a look at this book. We spent around forty-five minutes at the library. Then we walked to the ice cream shop, and I offered to buy her an ice cream. Sarah could see that I could look after a woman, that I was thoughtful and caring. She reckoned that I was a fine gentleman.

After having ice cream, Sarah accompanied me to the bus station. On the bus heading home, Sarah was ecstatic and couldn't wait for Saturday to come, which was the following day. The hug and kiss that Sarah gave me before she hopped on her bus made my heart leap. I caught the next available train to Cleveland and arrived at my apartment, exhausted but happy. I didn't feel like cooking so I ordered pizza from Eagle Boys Pizza, my favorite pizzeria. After having pizza for tea, I rehearsed the song that I intended to sing to Sarah for forty-five minutes. Then I read fifteen pages of my readings and called it a night.

Saturday morning came, and I had bacon and eggs for breakfast. I had a quick shower and put on something nice for my meeting with Sarah at the park. I caught the eight-thirty bus. There were about eleven passengers on the bus, all going into the city.

I got off the bus at the park. Sarah had arrived twenty minutes earlier from Red Cliffs. I knew that Timothy lived in a different suburb called North Lakes. He didn't know about the meeting at the park because it was just meant for Sarah and me, a meeting for two. It was a private meeting and only Sarah knew the real intent behind the meeting. To me, it was a meeting to showcase my talent. There would have been three of us if Timothy had been invited. Timothy was a bit overprotective of Sarah because they both came from the same country, and he considered her to be a sister.

"Hi, good morning, handsome," Sarah said and kissed me on the cheek for the second time. She wore high heels and her earrings look dignified. She grabbed my left hand and led me to a bench. I could feel heat like electric currents running through my hand, through my whole body. It felt good. There weren't too many people at the park. There was a lady walking her dog in the park, and a couple with their two kids watching about eight wood ducks in the lake, swimming in a pyramid fashion. A couple of sparkly swans also circled around in the lake. It was a perfect day to be at the park for a meeting of two.

I put my lunch box on the table and opened the guitar case, taking the guitar out. Sarah sat next to me with her legs crossed. "That's a nice guitar!" she exclaimed.

"It is. I haven't played it yet. It's Simon's guitar. I would like you to meet him and his gorgeous wife Jessica someday. I might ask them if you can come over for a barbie or something. They are a lovely couple. Jessica is like my mother. She is thoughtful and caring, like all mothers," I said.

"So are you going to play and sing for me today?" Sarah was impatient to hear my talent.

"I will try my best, gorgeous. For me, playing the guitar is still a learning experience."

"That's all right. It's good to be original and raw."

I hummed a gospel tune. I picked the strings, and it sounded like three different instruments playing all at once. It was harmonious.

"You are so good, Maduku! That's impressive! I am going to remember your music for a long time." Sarah said.

"Oh thank you."

"Are you sure, you haven't taken any music lessons? You sound professional. It's like you've been playing for a very long time at concerts and music festivals. Don't tell me that you haven't taken any music lessons at all!"

"No, I taught myself to play, and I practice, practice, practice," I explained. "Practice makes progress. There are so many dimensions, and you have to keep honing your craft to tap into those different streams and paradigms of music, those different layers, and levels."

"Can you play another one?"

"Sure!"

I played a contemporary tune this time. I had heard this tune on the airways back home. It has a bluesy feel to it. Sarah was snapping fingers and tapping her toes to my style of playing. She was enjoying herself and having a good time. She felt like all her troubles had just melted away in the moment. She found my music soothing to her soul. My music awakened her deep feelings for me. Her eyes showed she was possessed with lust for me. She got up and interrupted my playing. She pulled the guitar out of my hands and put it on the bench. Then she grabbed my head with her two hands, pulled it toward her, stooped down and landed a passionate kiss on my lips. She looked me in the eyes, her eyes drawn and welling with emotion. I could feel her lustful desires emanating through her eyes. It was so powerful. It numbed my soul.

Quickly, she moved to sit on my lap and locked her mouth to mine and landed another kiss, a sloppy one. She buried my face between her breasts and rubbed them across my face. Then she pulled away, still holding my head with her hands, muttering the words, "You are so talented. I want you." She kissed me again, bringing my face to her breasts. It was entrancing. I was a sheep to slaughter, powerless. A scream for help might have attracted the police, so I kept quiet and waited for the moment to break free from her grip. Sarah held my two hands on the bench and continued to kiss me. I struggled to free myself from her hands, but I couldn't.

Eventually, I managed to push her away. I was shaking all over. "What's the matter with you? This is wrong! I'm here just to sing for you as requested. This might get us into trouble if Timothy Kwairaga finds out," I said.

"So you mean that you don't love me? What's the point of singing a song and not expressing your feelings through the song?" Sarah was furious. "Come on! You should know that when a girl asks you to meet her somewhere, just you and her, that you are supposed to pick up the clues and the signs that she is giving you all along. That is how a woman communicates her feelings to someone she's interested in! What's wrong with you! What's the matter with you! You are single, and so am I! What trouble are you talking about? I've been sending you clues all along! I love you, Maduku!" Sarah said bursting into tears.

She buried her face in her palms and sobbed, repeatedly saying "I'm sorry" over and over. "I'm so sorry Maduku, I'm just a fool. I feel bad for myself right now. I feel so ashamed of myself," Sarah said. "You made me feel natural and special. Your music and singing brings joy and happiness to my soul. Women love to be entertained, and you did exactly that." Tears were streaming down her face.

Then she gently kissed me and said, "Have fun, and best of luck in life and in your future endeavors." She turned to walk away, but I grabbed her hand.

"Wait, Sarah! Wait! Please don't walk away from me like that! I'm sorry, I love you, but you just surprised me," I said. I grabbed her left hand and drew her close to me, kissing her madly and deeply. I kissed her, pulling her toward me with my left hand and caressing her back down to her waist with my right hand. I had crossed the line. I was sold to a beautiful woman. We left the park and escaped to South Island for a cruise around the island. It was a nice trip away from home.

Turning to her, I said, "I've never been kissed by a woman in my entire life. It's taboo in my culture. Shaking hands is deemed acceptable, especially with the opposite sex. Don't worry about the customs of my country, though. We are in a different country now, and things are done differently here. That's the ticket for exploring South Island in the future. Did you like South Island?"

"I love South Island; the view was beautiful," she said. "I told you it's a magical place. Would you like to go on a trip every now and again?" Sarah asked with a wink. The best time to explore the island is when it's wet, like on a rainy day. That's when all the nice fish come out looking for food and you can catch them, standing on the shore with your fishing rod.

"Thanks for the ride. Thank you for taking me there, Sarah."

"You're welcome."

The meeting at the park was over, and Sarah had captured my heart. We parted and caught our trains to our respective homes.

I headed home to Simon and Jessica's place to drop off the guitar.

"How did the meeting go, Maduku?" Jessica asked.

"It was fantastic! We had a good time. We plan to go to South Island for a vacation after our exams. My friend said it's beautiful out there. She's been there many times on her own," I said. "We might ask her friend, Mr. Timothy Kwairaga, to come with us if he's not busy."

"How did she get there? By plane or by boat? She must be rich to travel that many times by herself," Jessica said.

"She said she gets discounts every time she travels."

"Oh wow! I have visited South Island many times when Simon is away overseas on business or something. South Island has exotic beaches. The scenery and the greenery of the island are breathtaking. The view is beautiful down there in the south. It's the most visited island on the planet. But for some reason, most people who visit the island don't know about its magic. When they return, they lose everything. They lose their money, their careers, their leadership positions, and their businesses. They lose everything after visiting the south. My mum used to warn my brother when he was in college not to visit South Island until he finished college.

She thought it might derail him psychologically from his studies, and he might not graduate."

I went back to my apartment in Cleveland, but I couldn't sleep. I stayed up all night. Even though my eyes were closed, the adrenaline was flowing through my body like convection currents. I couldn't stop thinking about the delicate touch of Sarah's skin and the kisses from her juicy, wide lips. I yearned for more of her feeling and touch, and then I tried to figure out why people lost everything after visiting the island.

My relationship with Sarah shifted from being platonic to being intimate. Our souls were tied together. We took our hobby of memorizing scripture to another level. We used the pocket Bible to send little notes of love and scripture verses to each other. One of us would take the Bible home and then give it back the following day. We wanted to avoid any suspicion from Timothy Kwairaga.

# Chapter 12

# Brisbane Jail, Australia

In Australia, November is a beautiful summer month, and one warm Sunday afternoon, everything changed. It was raining heavily outside. Sarah and I, and some other students, including Timothy, were in the library, studying and writing our book reports. Sarah got up and went to the toilet. Ten minutes later, I got up and left the room, too. We were gone for about half an hour. A female student by the name of Hannah also needed some relief. She got up from her desk and went to the toilet. After she finished, she came out and saw me caressing Sarah, her back against the wall behind the library. We were lost in each other's eyes, and because of the noise from the heavy rain, we thought no one was around. Hannah didn't want to interrupt us, but she went inside and told Timothy that we were talking at the back of the building.

Timothy's first reaction was to grab Sarah's Bible and flip through the pages. He was shocked to see all the love letters that we had written to each other in the margins of the Bible. He was furious and headed out to confront me, the Bible in his hand. As we were still with our arms around each other, we didn't hear him coming when suddenly he appeared from the corner and threw the Bible on the ground in front of them.

"Here! What a load of crap I've found inside this Bible!" He was nearly yelling. Sarah pushed me away from her embrace, but it was too late. He had seen her wrapped in my arms, passionately kissing me. "I can't believe what you two have been doing,' he continued, "fooling and deceiving everybody, including me, with this scripture memory thing and going to church on Sundays!"

"What's your problem with me, Timothy? Are you jealous? You should mind your own business!" Sarah angrily said to him.

"We are both from the same country. I considered you as my sister. That's what our elders taught us, to care for our fellow countrymen and women in a foreign land!"

Sarah's eyes were blazing. "Yeah, I know, but this is a foreign country, and you are not my biological brother. This is my life, and I have the right to do whatever I want or date anyone I adore. Get the hell out of here!"

Timothy was furious and burned with anger. He approached me with his right fist clenched and threw a punch at my face. I blocked the blow with my left hand and placed my right leg on his groin and right knee. This caused him to lose his balance. With an uppercut to his chin with my right fist, I grabbed the back of his neck with my left hand. With my right hand on Timothy's left shoulder, I then pulled him forward, knocking him down with my right leg. Finally, I kicked him squarely in the head. All these actions happened within ten seconds and in the name of self-defense. Timothy was sprawled on the ground, face up in the pouring rain with a bleeding nose and a fractured jaw.

He was unconscious, and all he could see was stars in the pouring rain. He couldn't talk. Sarah stood by, shaking and crying, and the students in the library all came rushing out into the rain to see what had happened. Their shocked expressions said it all. "Ring the police! Ring the police to arrest him," they were saying. Hannah, the news reporter, called triple zero, and the police and ambulance came in no time at all.

Timothy was taken away on a stretcher and rushed to the hospital, where it was determined that he was in a coma. The police took down statements from the witnesses. The whole class seemed to be on Timothy's side, not mine. Since I had gotten involved with Sarah, they had not been exactly nice to me. Sarah was the centre of attention on the campus. She looked like a model, and her body was to die for. After the police finished talking to the students, I was handcuffed and taken into the police van. I was charged with assault and taken into custody. My classmates didn't see me again until my court hearing. I learned later that Sarah had left the library and walked to the bus station in the pouring rain. She was angry and ashamed.

The news of the fight spread like wildfire through the campus. Everybody was talking about it in astonishment. Sarah's secret and silent admirers were happy that I had been arrested. They had eagerly awaited for this day to come. Some prayed and actually thought that the incident had been an answer to their prayers. They didn't want to hear that I had married Sarah after college. They didn't want to see us walking around town, holding hands. Well, I guess their wishes came true. I had been expelled from college, and my future plans to graduate from college with a certificate or to marry Sarah were most in doubt and probably out of reach.

Police went to Simon and Jessica's place to tell them that I had been arrested and put in custody. They told them that I had gotten into a nasty fight with a fellow student, and I was due to appear in court on the 15th of December. I was being charged with assault and intentionally inflicting bodily harm on a defenseless person. Simon and Jessica were shocked and speechless. They could not believe what had happened. But Jessica had known all along, that sooner or later, if I continued to hang around with Sarah and feelings began to develop, I would get myself into trouble. And she was dead right. I was in trouble, locked away in custody, waiting for my judgment day to come.

December the 15th arrived. I dressed in long white pants and a t-shirt.

I was escorted out of the van by two police officers in black uniforms, and led into court to answer the judge about the charges against me. The students and my haters were also present in court to hear my judgment. Sarah was present, as was Hannah, the reporter with her witnesses which turned out to be nearly all the men in the class. Timothy was still in the hospital's intensive care unit, unable to attend court. The judge was going to make his judgment based on evidence provided by Hannah and her witnesses.

The claims that I acted in self-defense were rejected and found unsatisfactory by the judge. The judge sentenced me to jail time for two years. As I was led away to jail by the police officers, I heard Sarah crying. That was the last time I saw her. Hannah and the students who witnessed the fight never saw me again. In fact, I was never to be seen again. My academic journey had come to an end. Simon and Jessica, too, never saw me again after my judgment was read. Jessica saw Sarah in the courtroom and agreed that she was a fine, beautiful lady, capable of breaking a man's heart. Jessica had no doubt that Sarah had won my heart.

Hannah was ashamed for interfering into other people's business, and she left college after my sentencing. She went home without graduating. A short time later, she was found dead in her bedroom with three empty chloroquine packets beside her.

Sitting in jail, I felt that all the stars in my sky had fallen. The words of the old man I met on the ship who was traveling from his home island to the capital city popped into my head.

Don't negotiate or compromise and fall for a woman's advances or juicy words but flee before destruction overtakes you; fleeing is the only way to escape her trap, not standing and negotiating to her terms. She is a powerful negotiator, the ability to negotiate and command attention is inherent and natural in her design and makeup. And when she uses the most powerful weapon that she possesses in the process, which is her eyes, then it's over, it's done.

I was finally convinced that a woman is the deadliest, most dangerous and powerful creature on the planet. The good words I had heard from Brother Andrew also rang loudly in my head. The two problems that I had encountered in the village and for which I was seeking solutions also emerged from my mental file. It seemed as if the ghosts of the words and the problems I was trying to solve were visiting me in jail. They were painful memories, tormenting and utterly agonizing. I felt like I was caged in a fiery furnace with no escape. I was at the crossroads of my life. I didn't know if I was going to find the solutions at college or in the real world. It was still a question that I needed to answer.

In jail, I developed a new hobby: reading. I read an average of two to three books every week. Fiction or nonfiction. It didn't matter. I read them all during my time in jail. I asked for a notebook and a pen so I could journal, but it was prohibited because they feared that I might injure myself or hurt someone with the pen. After serving two years in jail, I was fluent in conversational English. I could give a speech without written notes. My large vocabulary was amazing. I was a living library of words walking on two legs. I did the time, and when the time came, I was ready to be deported back to my home country.

# Chapter 13

## Henderson International Airport, Honiara

On a Thursday morning, two police officers arrived at the jail, gave me some papers to sign, and led me to a waiting van, the same van that had taken me to jail after the judge had sentenced me. They took me straight to the airport, but they didn't take me through immigration like the other passengers. I was driven through another exit and led by the police officers to the plane. They ushered me into the plane, showed me my seat, and wished me a safe and enjoyable trip back home.

"Okay, mate, have a safe and enjoyable trip back home," one of the two officers said.

"Thank you, guys. Sooner or later, you'll see me on the big screen," I said.

The two officers had no clue what I was talking about. "Whatever that means. We wish you all the best in your future endeavors," they said as they left the plane. The passengers bet that I must have been arrested and was being sent home to face charges.

Sitting in my seat, looking through the window, I felt ashamed and really down in spirits. I remembered Jessica's words about South Island. It finally dawned on me what she meant when she talked about people who lost it all after visiting the island. I knew then that Jessica was right. South Island was the island of happiness, but also the island of sorrow and pain if you didn't take care. My visit to South Island had been one of the main reasons for my deportation from college.

I didn't know what to say to the elders in my community when I returned home. I felt like I had let my people and my community down. I was so ashamed. Thoughts of despair and self-condemnation started intruding into my mind. I thought about going into solitary confinement somewhere in the mountains on Guadalcanal when I got home. I felt it would be better for me to be dead. At least if I was dead, I wouldn't have to worry about being mocked and ridiculed by people in my village. But I decided I would go home first. Committing suicide because I didn't get the chance to marry Sarah or because I was expelled from college and deported was a permanent solution to a temporary problem. I didn't want people to remember me as the one who committed suicide for being deported from college. I reminded myself that it was not the end of the world. I just needed to sit down and allow the dust to settle so I could see what was left of my life. I could work with that reality and move forward.

From my seat in the plane, looking down on the clouds was not comforting. I didn't want to talk to the person sitting next to me. I didn't want to eat or drink anything, even though the meal was included with my ticket. As I was sitting my seat, battling thoughts of failure and depression, a flight attendant walked past. I stopped him and asked, "Excuse me, sir! Where is the tall lady with the long tanned legs and sparkling brown eyes? Does she still work for the airline?"

"I'm sorry sir, she died in a car accident a year ago. She was driving home from church when her car collided with another car. Do you know her? She was a rich lady and owned several rental properties in town," the flight attendant replied. "She was an only child, and her parents have been dead for many years. She was from the long island of Isabel where the locals say the angels of the country come from. Was she a friend or relation of yours?"

"No sir, I met her on this very plane. She gave me her contact details and begged me to get in touch. I was careless and dropped the card in a trash bin in the arrival lounge," I explained.

"Oh, boy, you threw away a great amount of wealth in the trash. The courts are searching for anyone with whom she keeps in contact, the next of kin, anyone, so they can transfer everything to that person's name. But they want evidence. Letters, birthday cards, some proof of her contacts and correspondence. To date, no one has come forward with any of that evidence.

"Close relatives and loved ones searched through her diaries and notes but found nothing about who she bumped into while she was flying on the plane. The only thing they found was a few words of regret she penned in the middle of her diary. She mentioned that she had given her contact details to a man who she admired and was attracted to, but she had never heard from him. They searched for a reply from the man for evidence of correspondence, but there wasn't any. She mentioned she met the gentleman on the plane. That's all they found," the flight attendant said.

"That gentleman was me, sir! I am the one! She did give me her contact details on a piece of paper, and I dropped it in the garbage bin in the arrival bay," I said, my eyes welling with tears.

"It's too late, sir. You chucked wealth into the trash, and now, no one will benefit from her wealth," he said.

Choking back tears, I told him how careless and stupid I had been.

"It's over, sir, you had your chance, and you blew it," he replied with little sympathy.

The airplane descended from the sky and finally landed and came to a stop. The doors opened, and the passengers and I disembarked and walked to the customs and immigration officials.

# Chapter 14

## In Honiara, the Capital City

No one knew that I had been expelled from the college and deported back home. Of course, no one was waiting for me at the airport. Even the sisters weren't there. It was as if I had no family and friends. I felt like a stranger returning home. Other passengers checked through customs and immigration and boarded a taxi. Some were picked up by family and friends, while some boarded public buses and headed into the city. Where they were going was anyone's guess.

I returned home with only the clothes I was wearing, but without money. I walked around in front of the airport building, going from one end to the other. The cabbies asked me if I was all right. I said I was waiting for a friend to pick me up, but I was actually lying to them to avoid being ridiculed for having just arrived from overseas and with no money. I didn't want to feel embarrassed. I didn't want them to know that I was returning home in disgrace, as poor as when I had left. I was hurt and wounded emotionally, like a deer limping along in pain in a dry and thirsty desert. I was broken. The whole experience burned like fire in my bones. Even though the face I showed was smiling, I was hurting tremendously inside.

Suddenly a woman in her mid-forties pulled up and offered me a lift. "Where did you want to go, young man? I can give you a lift to your destination," she said.

I declined at first, but she insisted. I jumped in, and we headed west on the highway to the city.

"Please take me to Sisters Martha and Mary's place," I said.

"Okay, no worries. By the way, I'm Nofu Atkins. I teach grammar at Oasis Grammar School, but I'm originally from the states. I'm single, never married. I don't know why. I guess I need to go out a bit more to meet people. My brother is an electrical engineer who brings light into people's homes. He has a five-year contract with a gold mining company that extracts gold and other minerals from the interior of the island. How do you know Sisters Martha and Mary?" she asked.

"Through a registered nurse who worked with them in my district, but I never met them personally. The sisters live on the hill, overlooking the harbor," I lied.

"Oh, I know the place you are talking about. I used to go to their church years ago, but I stopped because of misappropriation of church money, which is actually stealing in itself. They just used a different term to make it sound nice. But I can take you there on Sunday. You might be able to meet them if they are still active members after all those allegations labeled against the board. A few months ago, I ran into a friend while running errands in town, she told me the sisters have moved to a new location in the city."

This information worried me, and she could see the concern on my face. "Don't worry, I can take you to lodge with my brother and his family first, then I'll take you to church on Sunday. Is that alright with you if I take you to my brother's place first?"

"No worries. That's fine," I replied.

"But first, we need to get petrol at the service station near the bridge, and something to eat. Are you hungry?" Nofu asked.

"Yes, I am, I said. "I have a craving for fish and chips or something."

We pulled up at the station, and she put petrol into the car. Then she got fish and chips for me and for herself. The chips were hot and crunchy, and the fish was cooked well with less flour and oil, just like I liked it. As we sat eating our meal, Nofu asked, "So what sort of work did they do in your district? The sisters, I mean."

I told her they were nurses under the church mission on the island and elsewhere. Nofu was inquisitive and curious to know about my affiliation with Martha and Mary. She could sense the hurt and the pain inside of me. She could tell from my eyes and through my words that something was wrong. As a woman, she had an acute sense of awareness and sensitivity to what was happening deep inside my heart. She could even discern danger miles away. A woman is an incredible creature. Her intuition is unmatched.

"Actually, I never met them in person," I continued to lie. "I heard of them through a nurse who worked at White River Clinic at that time. She told me about the sisters. Both of them used to work as nurses in my district. When I got the scholarship to study at college, I needed a place to stay in the capital city to organize my visa and travel arrangements. This nurse helped me to lodge with the sisters at their residence. I stayed with them for more than two weeks, until I left for college. They were so helpful and supportive. Kind and lovely people. They were great cooks, too." I paused and took a deep breath, knowing that I needed to confess to my past.

"At college, I messed up," I continued. "I slacked off and lost focus and discipline. I got involved with a beautiful lady, a fellow student, and gave her everything: my values and standards that I believed in and embraced. I ended up in a nasty fight with a male student from the Caribbean, the same country she comes from. They knew each other from primary school and parted ways when they transitioned to junior high. He had some interest in this lady, but was too scared to take the risk to make it known to her. In the fight, I acted in self-defense, but he ended up in a coma at the hospital. The ambulance and the police came. They took him to the hospital, and the police took me to custody. I waited for my judgment from the judge for many days. Finally, judgement day came, and I was sentenced to two years in jail. I was libeled and slandered by students' who provided evidence, especially from the female student who caught us behind the library. I was charged with assault, did the time in jail, and was deported upon my release. It's a long story, but that's how I originally met the sisters," I said resignedly.

"I am sorry to hear that your academic journey was cut short like that! I believe the sisters moved, but I am willing and happy to arrange with my brother for you to lodge with him and his family until you are ready to travel back to your home island," she offered. I nodded in appreciation.

We left the station and headed into the city. "The city isn't safe anymore. It's dangerous to walk alone at night. Gone are the days when you could just sleep on the beach at night, look up into the sky, count the stars and listen to the roar of the ocean and the waves splashing on the shoreline. It used to be you could park your car along the street at night, and in the morning, it would still be there with all four wheels attached. Nowadays, if you park your car along the road or in the street at night, you return in the morning to find the wheels gone, the windows smashed, and the accessories in the car removed. Crime and violence are rampant in the city because of joblessness," Nofu said.

We arrived at her brother's place, and she got out to talk to her brother, explaining the situation. Her brother agreed to let me stay at his house until I was ready to go home. He was understanding and had a compassionate heart, just like his sister. Nofu went back to the car and said, "Alright, Maduku, grab your bag, and come meet my brother. I will go and buy something for tea in town, and I'll get back to see you tonight so we can have tea together."

I grabbed my bag and introduced myself to Nofu's brother.

"Hello, I'm George Atkins. Nice to meet you. Come on in and grab a chair. Have a seat," he said. After he made sure I was comfortable, he continued, "This is my beautiful wife, Nicole. She is my everything. She keeps my life grounded and makes me a better man. I love her with all my heart, soul, and mind. I love her with everything that is within me. She is my best friend and the mother of my only three children on the planet. She's the one who took my virginity."

"Yes, he's right about that," his wife Nicole said with a big smile. "This is our fifteenth year of marriage, happy and wonderful years. Do you want a cup of tea or something? What's your preference? Tea or coffee?"

"Just tea please, and one sugar," I said.

I could converse easily and with confidence to George and his wife. The American accent was a bit different to my ear, but I could understand what They were saying. After reading two to three books in a week in jail for two years, I had the words to use, even though I was hurting and broken on the inside.

Nofu returned from town with bread from the hot bread kitchen, sugar and butter, milk, and pizza, one of my favorite dishes. While we were having tea, Nofu explained a bit more about me to George and his wife. It was an emotional moment for me, having the Atkins family learn about how my academic journey and dream had been cut short. Nofu told them about the girl I fell for and that she ruined the whole thing for me, and that I eventually landed in an unthinkable mess. But they seemed accepting and understanding. They knew how hard it was for me to get into trouble in a foreign country. Eventually, the Atkins became my new family. Their kindness and generosity drew me into their lives. George sat me down one day, explaining a few things he had learned in life.

You know, Maduku, there is no success without failure. Failure means that you haven't got it right yet. It means that you probably need some more information for the project that you are working on. Learn from mistakes in life.

I am not a religious person, but my mother used to tell me about people in the Bible who messed up but eventually became successful, regardless of the mess and the setbacks they went through. She told me about Moses, who was a murderer and a fugitive. Did you know the first five books of the Old Testament were written by a murderer? She told me about David, a smelly shepherd boy who wrote the book of Psalms. His songs bring healing and comfort to the hurt and wounded. She told me of Saul, who later converted to Paul. He was a serial killer, but three-quarters of the New Testament was written by him.

Their stories give us hope that regardless of what we go through in life or how badly we messed up, the creator of mankind can turn all our mess into a wonderful testimony. Only the manufacturer knows his product better. There are two things I learned from these Biblical stories that my mother told me. First, I could use them as examples and warnings of what to do and what not to do. They serve as reference and precedence for us to see what outcome we want in our lives.

You can look around and see some of the successful men and women in our modern day and emulate the successful habits that they cultivate that made their very success possible. And you can also look around and see those who failed because of the lousy habits they cultivated. You get out of life what you put in. So take heart and be of good courage.

So what are your goals when you return to your village? Do you have anything particular in mind that you want to do? What kinds of opportunities are there in terms of natural resources and stuff like that? In the villages, most of the people are just subsistence farmers, working the land for their daily livelihood and survival. What else is there besides subsistence farming?

Feeding pigs would be a potential project worth venturing into because you don't need to invent pigs. They've been here since they were found on the earth, and caring for pigs is a tradition that has passed on from generation to generation. It takes about four to six months to see a return on your investment of time and energy, but it's worth it. The turnover far exceeds the time and energy invested. Another good thing about feeding pigs is that you can stay home, and you don't have to worry about paying bills on a weekly or monthly basis. You eat what you grow in your garden or behind your backyard, and it's free of chemicals or pesticides.

I think feeding pigs would suit you because you are keen to be successful in life. I, my wife, and Nofu will talk, then I will let you know the outcome of our conversation tomorrow. We have money tucked away in the bank for assisting people who want to make a difference in the world. It is not much, but we always consider our assistance as a mustard seed, when planted in the right environment, with patience and good management, it will grow and bring forth much fruit. It's a principle we have cultivated and lived by in everything we do. We believe in managing the little we have, knowing it will come back multiplied many times over.

"There is a high demand for pigs at Easter or Christmas time or when someone gets married or when a community inaugurates a priest or dedicates and sanctifies a new building for worship," I said. "Not only that, but when I was in primary school, my aunt assigned me the task of caring for the pigs. My aunt took care of me after my parents passed. In her list of daily chores, I was the one to feed the pigs before sunset every day, and I loved it. I loved hearing them grunt, running toward me in the pen for feed," I said.

"Then you are experienced, too," George exclaimed. "Even better!"

"I think I better go. It's getting late. I will see you all in the morning. Have a good night," Nofu said.

"Thank you for tea. It was really nice, especially the pizza. After such a long time away from eating it, it tastes different," I said.

"You are welcome," Nofu said, smiling as she got into her car. She turned the ignition and disappeared around the corner, headed east through the cemetery, where great men and women were buried with their thoughts, ideas, dreams, visions, inventions, innovations that never came to be, never came to materialize because of procrastination or laziness or lack of information. These people's dreams had died with them. They had never given birth to their brain child.

In the morning, Nofu arrived with three loaves of bread, hot and fresh from the Hot Bread Kitchen. While we were sitting around the table, Nofu said to me, "I don't know why I drove through the airport that Thursday afternoon. I didn't have any plans or intentions of driving through the airport. It's the school holidays. I initially intended to check the floral shop on the highway. While driving east toward the floral shop, I felt a very strong urge to drive to the airport. If I had disobeyed that urge, I might not have met you at the airport, and we might not have crossed each other's path. The thought of driving through the airport grew stronger and stronger, so I responded in obedience to that inner nagging. I knew the universe was saying something to me, and I needed to respond promptly, without questioning why I was being told to do so.

"Today, I want you to come shopping with me in town. We need to buy you a bush knife and a box of envelopes and stamps so you can write to us from the village. We would love to keep in touch and hear of your progress. We want to be a part of your story," Nofu said.

In town, we entered the big hardware store situated opposite the city mall. The locals in the shops were staring and wondering why a black bloke was following a beautiful Caucasian woman and carrying her shopping bag. Together, we walked to the aisle where the knives and axes were shelved.

" Do you use an axe in the village?" she asked me.

"Yes, I do. I use it for chopping wood for cooking and light," I replied.

Nofu grabbed a pair of gloves, jungle boots, a knife, and an axe. The knife and axe were made in Sweden. People in the village always bought things "Made in Sweden", especially when it came to knives and axes.

We took the items to the counter. A gorgeous young lady, probably in her mid-twenties, was the cashier. While she served us, she kept looking at me from time to time and smiling. Nofu noticed the cashier's body language, knowing that it was the way a woman expressed her emotional feelings and desires. She was a beautiful lady.

The cashier wondered if the good looking man worked for Nofu or if she might be a golfer and he was her caddie boy. That kind of relationship was common between the locals and Caucasian women who liked to play golf for recreational purposes.

Nofu paid for the goods, and we left. In the car, Nofu said, "I think she likes you, Maduku. I can tell by the way she kept looking at you while scanning the goods."

"Really! I don't know, but she comes from a region where dowry payment to marry a girl is a lot of money. A girl is worth more than a house or an automobile. My aunt warned me not to touch a girl from that region.

They are all the same, very expensive to marry. The dowry payment is unbelievable in that region. They charge too much for their girls," I said.

"How do you know she is from that particular region?" Nofu asked.

" Did you see that tattoo of the sun's sign on her face. That's their mark of identification. Every girl born has the sign of the sun tattooed or inscribed on her face," I explained.

"Yes, you right about that. I've seen the sign of the sun on many beautiful faces in town and at the market," Nofu said.

"About the dowry items, I've seen and read about it in the paper, and seen photos of traditional marriages with the bride, dressed in a blue skirt, her breast barely covered, decorated with armbands of bird feathers, with shell money diagonally wrapped from her shoulders to her waist. She is a costly and prized possession, above everything else, even more expensive than the price of real estate," I said. "I'm not sure if I have the ability to touch one from that region in the future."

We went to the post office to buy some stamps and envelopes. There were some beautiful women at the post office. Their smiles were infectious. As we were leaving, one of them actually ran outside to see which direction we were heading. Those in the post office were wondering about the connection I had with this beautiful Caucasian woman. Women from the hardware and the post office were noticing me. They were curious and inquisitive, wondering where I was going with Nofu.

Another day passed, and we returned to George's house, having done our shopping. Nofu, George, and his wife talked in the kitchen while I watched basketball on a video tape in another room. George and his family were keen followers of the NBA.

After chatting for about twenty-minutes, they came in and told me that they were going to give me some financial assistance to get me started.

"Maduku, we've talked and collectively agreed and decided as a family to assist you on your new path with some financial investment. I will give you the envelope with the money inside when you're ready to board the ship back to your home island," George said. "We believe in good faith that with what little you learned at college about management, you will apply that information to your new venture to make the money grow many times over. "We are believers in managing what little you have into the dream, the vision, the ideas life has given you. We want to see your tree bring forth fruit in abundance. We want to partake and share in your success and your story."

"I want to contribute to what George just said. Remember that it is possible to achieve your dream. The path has never been even. The road to success is rocky and hilly, and you will encounter setbacks and detours along the way, but remember this, 'If it is hard, do it hard.' Surround yourself with people who are going somewhere, who have a dream. Avoid toxic and cynical people who can sabotage or destroy your dream. People will laugh, mock, and ridicule you. They will call you names and say all kinds of things, but remember, they will announce your victory and sing your praises from the mountain top. They will cheer for you when you score the goal from the sidelines. Just leave them waiting and watching to see what you can do with the mess you've gone through. Your cynics will condemn and criticise and mock you from afar, but don't you worry about them. You get to work and stay on course this time," Nofu said.

"Thank you very much for the words of hope and encouragement that you have shared with me. I never thought I was ever going to get up again after the mess I've gotten myself into. You people were the beacon of hope and light in the darkest moment and hour of my life, a time when everything seemed so dark, a time when no sunshine or rainbows brightened my world, a time when it seemed that all the stars in my sky had fallen," I said, choking back the tears. Nofu embraced me, reassuring me that it was going to be all right.

"It's never too late to live your dreams, young man. Be a mighty man of valor. Be brave and courageous. As long as you are breathing, you can do it, if you never give up," Nofu said.

Friday evening had come, and it was time for me to leave the capital and travel to my home island on the boat. Ms. Nofu, her brother, and his wife went with me down to the wharf to see me off.

"It was a pleasure meeting you, Maduku. A coincidence has turned into a friendship with our family. Strangers became friends. It feels like we have known you for ages!" Nofu said.

"It was a pleasure, really, to meet you through my sister," George said. "We are family now. Hearing about your story and what you have gone through was overwhelming but inspiring. Your resilience and the courage to look life in the eye, saying it is not over until I win, is just amazing. There are only a few people who could have handled what you've gone through. Most people aren't built to deal with such difficulty. I really admire the tenacious and audacious spirit that you have. I enjoyed talking with you.

"You process and think about your thoughts before you speak. You pay very careful attention to the words you are going to say. You seem to understand the power of words and their effects on people's lives. I predict great things are going to happen to you. You will be amazed! A bright future is waiting for you to seize and own it. But you have to put in the work and the discipline to realize that future," George said. "Here is our gift to you. You have demonstrated a tremendous potential to turn your life around by sharing with us your vision for living, and it is now up to you to make the most of this opportunity. It is not much, but with patience, perseverance, and determination, you will reap the harvest."

They each hugged me, and I turned to board the ship.

"Please keep in touch, we would love to know of your progress", Nofu said. The Atkins family was going to miss me a lot, and I was going to miss them.

The captain announced that all who were onboard and not intending to travel had to leave the ship immediately. "This is the final warning call. Passengers who are visiting and not traveling with us, please leave the vessel now." The mooring lines were taken off the bow lines. The ship's engine reared up, creating bubbles and digging up debris from the seafloor. The ship moved out from the wharf. My new friends, standing on the wharf, waved as the ship turned toward the open sea. Nofu was emotional, her eyes welling up. And George and his wife seemed very sad to see me leave as well.

The passengers on the top deck of the ship shouted and waved to their friends and loved ones still on the wharf. Some of them were excited to escape from the mundane and boring routine of city life, going to work in the morning and getting home late, just to make a living, pay bills, and die. For me, I was going home with a mission. I had obligations and responsibilities to execute, and I knew I didn't have any time to squander. This time I was going to make sure that I utilized every second. The minutes and hours of my day had to be productive.

I decided to forget my past mistakes and failures, instead moving toward the future with a renewed purpose and vision. I didn't want my past to interfere with the future. At George Atkins house, I had made peace with my past and then solemnly put it to rest. I was more determined and driven than ever before to deliver the solutions to the compelling problems that drove my very existence.

The shoreline disappeared in the distance as night was falling, and the passengers fell asleep like dead men. The city lights appeared dimmed and then faded as the ship navigated through the waves in the dark. Sitting close to the ship's chimney, I settled down in the warmth and went to sleep like the rest of my shipmates. I was awakened by the crew checking for tickets, but then could not go back to sleep.

In the dark, I thought about how far I had come and how many miles I had traveled. I reminded myself that failures and mistakes are lessons to learn and retool for maximum impact. But I also felt the pressure of how the people back home would react when they saw me again. That pressure is the incubator for progress, growth, and development. One cannot grow in good times. Pressure and hard times reveal the true nature and essence of a man. It determines what he is made of and the strength of who he is. I felt that the ultimate purpose for the tough times I had had in life was to test me.

I had succumbed and failed in college, but I had also learned from that experience and promised myself to pursue my dream no matter the cost. I decided I wouldn't cast my eyes on another girl until I achieved my dream. Reaching these conclusions made me even more grateful. I pledged to keep a positive attitude and outlook when confronted with cynicism and doubt from the people back home in the village. Perhaps for the first time, I experienced humility, which surely must be the hallmark of maturity.

When I thought of those who had showed compassion and understanding during my darkest hours, I remembered the Atkins family, especially Ms. Nofu who had found me at the airport when I was at my lowest. Their positive attitude and how they had helped me pick up the pieces of my life and reassemble it, sharing their finances and offering words of encouragement and unyielding hope.

I found myself crying, tears streaming down my face. The kind gestures shown to me by perfect strangers—the Atkins family and the sisters of the church—would stay with me for life. I was grateful that in failure I had been given the privilege of meeting the Atkins family. Meeting them was the best thing that had ever happened to me. They bestowed their trust in me by sharing some of the principles that they had learned and applied in their lives that had made them successful in business and in life. They told me that with dedication, drive, determination and consistent pursuit of my dreams, I would bring those dreams to life. For all that I was grateful, I sobbed alone in the dark. But no one was watching. Those people around me were tending to their own lives, telling stories of their great losses and miraculous successes.

They were talking about a venture that hadn't worked out due to poor market research. They were discussing what it would feel like if everybody could realize their dreams before they left the planet. They listed the empty promises made in the halls of power by political representatives. They were talking about national projects that never materialized because of greed and jealousy and mismanagement of funds allocated by the government. I heard them voicing their concerns while I sobbed in the dark.

I finally went back to sleep having sobbed my sorrow into exhaustion. I woke up when the ship passed the Alitee reef, a reef speculated to have oil deposits. Unofficial reports claimed the oil had spilled and was endangering marine ecology in the vicinity of the reef. This kind of report excited people who prefer leisure over work, who invest in pyramid schemes, dreaming of becoming instant millionaires without any sweat and toil. Such speculations spread like wildfire in the small town and the villages nearby. I knew it would breed laziness and idleness among the people in the communities who claimed ownership of the reef. As we passed the reef, the captain announced from the wheel room that we would be docking in approximately in an hour.

After the announcement was made, people gathered their belongings, making sure they had everything with them before leaving the ship. The lights from the small town on the little island grew closer and closer, shining brighter as the ship approached the passageway to the wharf. People from the top deck of the ship started making their way downstairs. There was commotion, laughing and talking, people waking up and standing along the rail, taking in the morning breeze as it skirted past them, so soothing and refreshing to their skin. As the ship cruised into the passageway, passing thatch houses illuminated by hurricane lanterns, I recalled how some had withstood severe storms and hurricanes for years, and were still standing firm, even on artificial architectural landscaping.

The ship headed toward the wharf, and mooring lines were thrown and tied to the bow lines. The wharf was jam-packed with men, women and children, waiting for family members, friends, and loved ones returning home. Some had come to the market to sell fresh produce like bananas, vegetables, cassava, pineapples, and avocados. Some had come to the market to check the prices of goods similar to what they were growing back home, to encourage them to keep growing what they were growing because it would lead to high profits.

Some had come looking for a soulmate. The marketplace was an ideal spot to find a soulmate. It was where the beautiful, young people of the villages came together. They each had made their journey to the market to find their special one. It was the place to see and be seen.

Some had just come to the small town to see the ship and her passengers. It was quite interesting to wonder what brought people to the small town, especially on a Saturday. The passengers disembarked the vessel like ants crawling back and forth, carrying their luggage to the waiting passenger trucks. The truck owners were excited because the greater number of passengers meant more money for them in truck fare.

# Chapter 15

## Asi Asi Village, Ramos Island

I left the vessel and walked through the crowd to where the passenger truck parking was located, and boarded the one passing through my village. It was a blue Isuzu three-tonne truck.

"Are you passing through Asi Asi village, sir?" I asked the truck driver.

"Yes I do, all day every day except Sunday because it's the Lord's day," he replied. I jumped on board, joining thirty passengers sitting on the trailer at the back.

It was normal to sit at the back of the trailer. This truck usually carried thirty or more passengers on a very busy day. The driver had mastered the detours and the bends and the blind spots along the road. He hadn't had an accident in forty years, carrying large numbers of passengers on a regular basis, and sometimes bags of copra and cocoa. The road wasn't paved, of course, and during a heavy rainfall season, a pond appeared on the road, causing erosion and making it difficult for trucks to travel to the little town. During the rainy season, it rains three to four times every week, overflowing the rivers and increasing the forest density on the island.

The truck was full of men, women, and children. Amidst the passengers, a mother was crying because her son couldn't get medical attention and care at the hospital. The doctors were sending them home and said the boy had only three weeks to live. It was heartbreaking to hear.

Still another passenger, a young girl, was going to attend the funeral of her father who had been killed during a dispute over a logging operation in her village. She said her father was not a green activist but believed that everybody should do their bit to keep the planet safe by applying sound management practices in harvesting the earth's resources. He told her that it was important to leave the planet a little better than when we first found it.

Another mesmerizing passenger was a teacher at a junior high school in the capital. She was going home to be married to her high school sweetheart. Her marriage had been arranged and was one of intermarriage. Intermarriage has created wonderful relationships between families. It creates understanding and tolerance of another's culture and differences. She said that arranged marriage is a beautiful thing and highly respected by her people. In her community, the wisdom of the parents is invaluable and priceless, she explained. They chose a spouse for her based on hard work and character. They looked for certain qualities possessed by the significant other, and relied very little on beauty and charm.

"Beauty and charisma are superficial, temporary," she said. "They can burn under pressure, and will fade with the passing of time. We believe that true beauty is within."

Still another passenger was a fine young man who had just graduated from college. He had managed to finish college. His sole purpose of going home was to build a tombstone on his grandfather's grave. He was raised by his grandfather when he was in primary school. His grandfather had passed while he was away at college, studying for his teaching diploma in Social Science and English. He wanted to honor his beloved grandfather for the sacrifices he had made to make his dream come true.

The passengers traveling with me were fascinating. They were people with a mission. They know why they were going home. They weren't going home for the sake of simply going home. They were going home because there was work to be done. That night, there was no rain, and the sky was beaming with stars shining down on the earth. The moon was going below the horizon. Another new day was dawning. The truck crossed the longest bridge and came to a stop. I got off and paid my truck fare. It was still dark and very cold. I had arrived home at three o'clock in the morning.

I walked along the rugged road that had been built with the sweat of my people. It had been partially funded by the European Union, but it wasn't paved. The frogs croaking in the small stream running through the drainage of the road was the only sound I heard. There was no dog in the village to bark at strangers who entered uninvited.

I arrived at my aunt's house, and stood there wondering what her response would be when she saw me. But first I needed to let her know that it was I that had arrived. I realized that in the dark I was an unknown man arriving without my aunt's knowledge. I knocked on her door, and the lights came on. She was understandably nervous and hesitated to open the door.

"Knock! Knock! It's me, Maduku," I said.

"Excuse me, who are you again?" she said through the door.

"It's me, Maduku, who went to university to study."

She couldn't believe that I was knocking on the door. She quickly opened the door and hurried me inside. "Come on in, please. It's cold outside. What happened, Maduku? It's not time for the holidays yet. Why have you come home? You haven't come home for two years. Yet you never wrote to explain why you were not coming home for the holidays. I have been worrying the whole time about you. I thought you were dead or something. There was no letter, nothing from you. I was left in the dark wondering what in the world had happened to you."

"I've messed up big time, Aunty. I let you and the whole community down. I let everybody else who believes in me down. I was expelled from college after I was released from jail. I've been in jail for two years. That's why I didn't come home for the holidays. I was involved in a fight over a beautiful lady. She trapped me and drew me into her web. I sold out. I gave into her at a park. I sold everything: my values and my standards for some temporary gain. And in court, I was slandered and libeled by a female student who caught us behind the library. This lady, who contributed to my deportation, tricked and lured me into her religious pastime of scripture memorization. I thought she was a Christian girl and had honorable intentions, but she didn't. I was just a fool to fall into her trap. After my downfall, I realized that a woman really is a cunning creature, the most powerful and deadliest creature to ever walk the earth," I said. "I met an old man on the ship when I first traveled to the capital to organize my traveling arrangements. He warned me to keep a distance and not compromise or negotiate with a woman. I was naïve and succumbed to her beauty, wrapped in lust and religious camouflage. I was honest, but she wasn't. I am just a fool. I should have heeded the old man's warnings. I'm so sorry, Aunty. I've transgressed against you and the community and the very people who believed in me. I am no longer worthy to call you my aunt. Just treat me like a servant in your house," I cried. The way she looked at me, disheartened. I thought she might never look at me again, but then she spoke.

"Oh, my goodness gracious me! I am ashamed, Maduku. You bring disgrace to my name!" she said while choking back the tears. "I don't know what to tell the chief and everybody in the community. You bring disrepute to our family. You have betrayed the trust bestowed on you by the people and the chief and me, your aunt. I can't believe you've done this terrible thing. I've never been sad until today. Today is the saddest day in my life.

"You have done the unthinkable. Anyway, the damage has been done. There is nothing we can do about that. There's no point crying over spilled milk. And most of the time, we are to blame for ignoring the signals. We go into a particular situation with our eyes open. We are not blind. We know what we are doing. To say we don't know what happens is unacceptable and lame. We are not blind. It's different when you are under the control or influence of alcohol or something.

"However, the fact that you are still alive and breathing right now proves that you have some unfinished business to do. That dream is still inside of you, and it needs to be planted in the right environment. Coupled with the right ingredients, your tree will manifest with its fruits. I believe that environment determines destiny. Going overseas to college, in my opinion, was meant to help you find the missing link to your dream. And when you found the missing link, you bring it home and assemble the whole thing together. Your life, Maduku, was missing something. You thought the missing link might have been overseas, so you went overseas to find that missing part and bring it home to fix what needs to be fixed. That's my opinion about going abroad.

"So you initially hoped to find the missing part of the dream in your heart at college, in a formal environment, but it turned out tragically. So let's look around here at home. We might be able to assemble the whole thing here with what we already have available on the ground and within our reach, and we can incorporate it with the little bit that you learned at college. First, I will go and tell the chief in private that unfortunately you've been expelled from college. And he will find a suitable time to call everybody and explain to them what happened, and for you to render a public apology to the people. Being expelled from college is not the end of the world. It's not the end of your life. However, it is the end of your journey in the education system. But the dream is still inside of you.

"Life is interesting you know; it has its own way of visiting each and every one of us. It teaches each one of us the lesson we need to learn, especially if we didn't learn it the first time. Life takes us back to the class that we missed."

Early in the morning, around five thirty, when everybody else was still sleeping, my aunt visited Mr. Augustine Fanualama, the village chief. She went to his house and told him that I had returned home. She explained that I had been expelled from college over some girlfriend business. The chief's heart ripped. He couldn't believe what I had done.

"This is gut wrenching! Why did he do it? This is treason! This is a betrayal of trust bestowed on him by me and the people of this community! He was our beacon of hope and the light to our path. This is disgraceful and a shame. He is selfish and self-centered and has tarnished the image of this community," he said, his eyes welling with tears.

The chief wept bitterly and refused his wife's attempts to comfort him. He sobbed and sobbed for hours until his eyes were sore and swollen. The entire village was waking up and could hear his lamentations. They all thought that someone had died. Indeed, I could hear the wailing of the chief from his aunt's house. I was so ashamed of what I had done. I knew right away that the chief was overwhelmingly saddened to hear of my unfortunate experience at college.

"I've had my fair share of tears already this morning. I wanted to go into hiding somewhere, probably in the mountains or by the coast. This is shameful and disgraceful," Rose Mary said to Mr. Fanualama.( This is aunt Rose Mary talking to the chief)

"Thanks for letting me know. I will call a meeting tomorrow evening so that healing can take place quickly. I know everybody will be hurt when they hear this. This is not personal. It's not about Maduku. It's about the community and is a public issue," Mr. Fanualama said. "The community is entitled to know what happened because Maduku is a member of our community. It's like the human body. When the left hand or right leg suffers, it affects the whole body."

Ms. Rose Mary went back to her house and made me breakfast. It was made with love regardless of the hurt that I had caused her. She served me leftovers from the previous night's dinner: boiled cassava and taro leaf baked with beans, shallot, tomatoes, and coconut cream. She prepared it in a bamboo and warmed it on the fire. There was no power and refrigeration, and this was a traditional way of preserving food. It had been handed down from generation to generation.

To preserve cooked food, the meal is wrapped in leaves or stored in bamboo. The bamboo is uniquely designed in such a way to preserve food for months without it spoiling if regularly warmed on the fire every day. Pork can be stored in a bamboo for a fortnight or so. The natural scent of the bamboo tantalizes one's taste buds when the bamboo is cut open. There is no need to add garlic or other spices to make the pork taste great. The bamboo does it all. Bamboo is free and accessible, and there's no power or manual operational instructions to operate the bamboo tree.

The next day arrived, and I heard the chief blowing the conch shell, calling everyone to congregate at the house of meeting. This is where the village held meetings about issues affecting people's lives and the community. Young and old would come out from their thatch houses, walking barefoot on clay, with no thongs or shoes, laughing, whistling, and humming a tune as they walked to the house of meeting to hear why the chief had called them together. As the village arrived at the house of meeting, they noticed how sad and pale the chief's was. They knew it had to be serious to see him like that.

"Thank you, everybody, for coming. The reason for this urgent meeting is to inform you all that our son, Mr. Maduku Mamata, has been expelled from college because of trouble over a girl, and he has returned home. I am sad and heartbroken. I wanted to make you all aware so that when you see Maduku walking through the village to collect water or going to church for devotion before night falls, don't be shocked or hesitate to say hello to him. I have arranged for all of us to formally welcome back our son Maduku into the community. Please join us on Sunday. You can cook something so all of us can share. Maduku will render his personal apology to all of us at that time. That's what the blowing of the conch shell was about," Augustine said.

Everyone was shocked to hear the news. It was totally unexpected, and they were as heartbroken as my aunt. Soon, this terrible news would be heard loud and clear, and would spread like wildfire in the district that

I, the beacon of hope for Asi Asi village was expelled from college. There was complete silence in the house of meeting. Tears of sorrow and sadness streamed down people's faces. This shocking news was like cancer to their bones. Where once it had been encouraging and uplifting, it was now depressing and disheartening. My friends and neighbors sat in the house of meeting with heavy and bleeding hearts.

Breaking the silence, a widow, choking back tears said, "There is nothing more we can do about it. What is demanded of every one of us now is to seek a new way of moving forward! At the end of the day, he is still our son! What he has gone through does not cancel his identity and future. The fact that he is alive and breathing is proof that life isn't done with him yet. Everybody fails and makes mistakes at some stage in their lives. But it's important not to sit on the sidelines nursing your wounds and feeling sorry for yourself. You have to get up and get back into the race of life." The words of the widow touched everyone's heart.

As long as you are human, you will make mistakes. Making mistakes is part of the learning process.

The chief stood up and expressed his sincere gratitude for the timely and priceless words that the widow had shared. "Thank you so much for those words of hope and encouragement. They are like medicine to the soul, and we all need that at this difficult time. Don't forget that an evening tea will be held in the house of meeting on Sunday, next week. Everybody is invited, and please bring something to share if you can. This is to welcome back our son Maduku, regardless of what happened. We will give him an opportunity to speak and explain himself. He probably learned something out of his situation that he wants to tell us about. Thank you for your time and patience, and have a pleasant evening, and good night everyone," our chief said.

The people of the village walked back to their homes, still hearing the words of the widow ringing in their heads, for they were words of wisdom and hope. The sentiments she had shared were priceless. The wisdom she demonstrated in addressing and bringing comfort to the village at a difficult moment was indescribable. She had the ability to bring comfort and peace to the wounded and hurting.

A couple who attended the meeting found it hard to go to sleep. They stayed up all night, talking about the pearls of wisdom imparted by the widow. They had been married for twenty-two years and had never heard anyone with that wealth of experience and depth of wisdom articulate it so well. The husband even said he had attended many occasions—wedding ceremonies, funerals, or a farewell party—and not one single speech read during those occasions had ever come close to what the widow so eloquently and masterfully relayed in her remarks to the people. She was absolutely brilliant. Everybody was deeply touched and moved.

The next morning, two of their friends from the same village came over to visit expressed that they had been thinking the same things. They had also stayed up until dawn, thinking about the widow's words. They had been married for forty-two years and had six grandchildren.

They said that they had a friend who was a teacher and had studied at a prestigious university overseas. He had his masters in economics and business administration. They had listened to him speak at a funeral and had found it boring and empty, without emotion. He didn't know what to say at such a difficult moment, and he wasn't able to offer words of comfort, peace, and hope to those who had lost their loved one. They felt that the mourners had gone home dissatisfied. The couple said they were a little bit embarrassed because the speaker was their friend, and in their opinion, he could have done a better job of preparing his sermon. But they noted during their visits to his house that he often spent time playing Uno with the village folks, and listening to reggae and island music. His pastime activities seemed out of line with his profession. Yet both couples had been highly impressed by the widow's remarks about me.

Sunday evening arrived, and it was time for the evening tea to welcome and restore me back into the community. My aunt Rose Mary brought a ripe banana, avocados, sugarcane, and pineapple. She also brought baked yam and taro. They weren't required to, but out of the generosity of their hearts, the people of the village brought whatever they had available in their homes. The chief and his family cooked six chickens and two tuna fish. Once again, everyone assembled at the house of meeting. My aunt called to me to come and join the rest of the village. When I arrived, there was complete silence in the house. I sat down beside the chief who was dressed in black from head to toe. When it came to clothing, he loved everything black.

The chief stood very slowly and looked at his beloved community. Then his eyes stopped on me. Taking a deep and solemn breath, he said, "I would like to thank each and every one of you for coming. Tonight is particularly about welcoming and restoring Maduku back into the community. In spite of what happened, he is still our son. He is still a vital member of our community. We don't want hurt feelings to exist here. His aunt Ms. Rose Mary spoke with me last Saturday, and she told me that Maduku wanted to offer a public apology to all of us for what he has done. Maduku is here now, in our midst. So while you are enjoying your food, I want you to listen very carefully to what is going to be said. We gather to affirm our love and support to you, Mr. Maduku. We want you to know that regardless of what happened, you are still a son of the community.

"To be honest, you have hurt many hearts including mine. Your behavior was a betrayal of trust bestowed on you by the people and by me, the chief of Asi Asi community. This evening, we have gathered to resolve our grievances and hurt feelings and seek forgiveness from each other so we can move forward as a community and as a people. We don't blame you for what happened. Only you know what happened and how you got yourself into that situation. Our precious people here have asked me to convey their grievances as well as their forgiveness toward you despite what you have done. They know that we are human and no one is perfect. We all have made mistakes at some stage in our lives. So this evening, I declare that you are forgiven and free to walk around in the community without guilt, fear, or condemnation. Whoever I set free is free indeed.

Welcome home."

There was a round of applause from the people, and I shook the chief's hands in appreciation of his cordial and warm reception. I tried to look at the audience, but I found that I couldn't bear to see the sadness and disappointment in their eyes. For what seemed an eternity, I looked down at my dusty feet, never saying a word. Without warning, tears began streaming down my face. I knew the moment of truth had arrived.

"Thank you, Chief Augustine. Thank you, everybody. First let me say that I am sorry for what I have done. I have betrayed your trust and let you down as a community and as a people. I take full responsibility for what happened. I was selfish and prideful, putting my needs and self-interests ahead of the communal aspirations and endeavors we collectively seek to achieve. I am deeply sorry for what I have done, and I sincerely accept your forgiveness as conveyed by Mr. Augustine, our chief," I said choking back the tears.

The chief's wife got up and embraced me, patting my shoulder and assuring me that all people make mistakes and unfortunately mistakes are part of life. She told me that I was doing the right thing, apologizing to the village and begging forgiveness from the people. I knew that the people had forgiven me.

Once the chief's wife concluded her embrace and stepped back from me, all the people in the house of meeting cheered and applauded me for being brave and honest. Asking for forgiveness was a sign of humility. It meant knowing what I had done was unthinkable and uncalled for, and I should have avoided it at all costs if possible. Saying sorry was the right thing to do because I was part of the community. My success was everybody's success. My failure had been everybody's failure.

I felt again that I was a team member who could play a vital role in moving the community forward to maximize its potential and realize its destiny. When I had messed up, the whole community had suffered. I knew an apology to the community was necessary and healthy for the social development of the community. It was a reminder to everyone, young and old, to always endeavor to stay on the high road and do the right thing, even when nobody was watching. It was a commitment to hold oneself accountable to the values on which the success of the community relied: mutual respect, hard work, and honesty.

When one chooses to tamper with the values the community holds dear, his success or failure is a public issue, not a private one. One's behavior in private and in public portrays and reflects the image of the community. It is all one and the same. When one member succeeds, everybody rejoices. When one member suffers, everybody mourns. Success is not a personal issue in the community. It's a public issue.

# Chapter 16

# I Find Love and Settle Down

A couple of weeks passed, and one night after the evening tea, I had a serious and constructive talk with my aunt. I explained to her that I wanted to venture into raising pigs like I had done when I was in primary school.

"I have a little bit of money given to me by a family from the states. Their family name is Atkins, Ms. Nofu Atkins and her brother, George. They live and work in the city. Nofu is single, but she's still hoping to meet the one. And her brother is an electrical engineer, and he's doing very well. Nofu is a teacher. She teaches grammar at Oasis Grammar School. Without know why, one day she was called to make a trip to the airport, and there, she found me in all my sadness and shame. She gave me a lift to town, and she asked me where she should take me. I mentioned Sisters Martha and Mary, the sisters of the church living on the hill overlooking the harbor. She said she heard they had moved to a new location. She suggested lodging with her brother and his family until I was ready to go home. I have no doubt that it was divine intervention. I was down and broken, cold and lonely inside, when she found me. I agreed and I stayed with George and his family right up to the day I left the capital.

"They were like family to me. I told them my story, my dreams, and my hopes for the future and my unfortunate experience at college. They were understanding and compassionate people. In the Atkins family, honesty is the only policy. It is one of the fundamentals that they embraced and built their lives upon over the years. They practice what they preach, and you can see it in everything they do. They have no ulterior motives in dealing with people. They think that all others are like them, too. I can tell you that they are different. Ms. Nofu bought me an axe and a knife, and stamps and envelopes for corresponding. They asked me to keep in touch because they want to visit me in the future to see what I'm doing.

"Ms. Nofu is different from many people her age. She is mature and sees the end from the middle or even in the beginning. She moves into the future with a plan, and has the ability to predict the future of people by how they wisely use their time. She said to me, 'How people use their time determines whether they are going to succeed or not in what they are doing. Time is a commodity given equally to everybody. Everybody has the same number of seconds, minutes, and hours in a day. How people effectively maximize their time allotments determines how far in life they will go. Time is the currency of life. The amount of time you have to trade determines how much value you are going to receive in return.' She was a very smart lady," I said.

My aunt was spellbound, listening to Nofu's wisdom and insight. "She really is a one of a kind woman. So different. Her words spell out her maturity and wisdom. I have never heard life's philosophy spoken so elegantly," Rose Mary said.

"Her brother George is another character. He doesn't talk too much and has a quiet personality. He is five foot, two or three inches tall with clear eyes and an easy smile. He is a man of great integrity who is committed to using his gifts to bring light into darkness and into people's homes. He loves his wife more than she loves him, and his wife knows it so well. His loyalty and undivided attention to his wife are unquestionable. His wife is the most important person in his life, above all else. Her happiness is his priority. He couldn't wait to go home to his wife every day after work. For George, going home is a great joy. He loves his family so dearly. His wife and children are his precious jewels and possessions," I continued. "He is careful and mindful of what he says to his wife. He knows that she is like an incubator, an emotional one.

"She receives things and processes them on an emotional level. George understands his wife, and his wife encourages and supports him in his work. She is the bedrock of their family and the love of his life. She never says anything bad or insults her husband in front of her kids or in public. She recognizes that George is the authority in the home, and he also serves as her protector. They've had their moments, but she knows her boundaries. She has never overstepped them.

"Mrs. Atkins is also an ambitious and industrious woman. She just shines at whatever she puts her heart and soul into. This is probably because of George's supportiveness and his willingness to bring out the best in her. Sometimes she cooks food for the people who work for her husband in their family business. She weaves and knits cotton baskets and sells them. She is mindful of her dressing and what she wears, but she dresses to be comfortable. She knows that what she wears is a reflection of her husband's image, both in private and in public. She dresses to earn and command respect. She doesn't dress as if she looking for other men to admire her. The only admiration she wants is from her husband in private. In public, she is a virtuous woman with grit and standards. She understands that respect is never a given, that it must be earned. She earns that by the way she dresses and talks. George is so blessed to have found her. She is a perfect example of a woman with class and standards," I said.

"You certainly were observant, and you remember every detail of the Atkins family," Rose Mary said.

"Yes, I saw it first hand during my short stay with them," I replied.

"That's a good life lesson for you. You have seen the teamwork between a husband and wife, how to treat and support each other like team members. Marriage is teamwork," she said. "Poor Nofu, it's just a bit unfair and sad that she hasn't met a good man like her brother George.

"Now, I will start you off with two pigs, a male and a female. That is my investment into your vision. Use the money the Atkins family gave you to buy feed. You may want to hire the soccer club to clear the bush behind our house to grow pumpkins to supplement the pigs feed," she said.

I started off with the two pigs, a male and a female. The two pigs became productive and gave me twelve piglets which I kept. For a second time, the female got pregnant, giving birth to another twelve piglets. I kept all of them, and I was very busy and didn't have time to play soccer or hang around with the other young men in the area.

As time went on, I sold a few pigs and earned good money for them. I tucked most of the money away in a savings account in the bank, bit I bought a mountain bike, a Chicago Bulls cap, and a pair of RM Williams boots with the rest. Those boots were handsome, the kind blokes love to wear, and I walked around in the market so people could see me.

He kept feeding, breeding, and selling my pigs until one day I reached the stage where I needed an assistant. But I was reluctant to seek a helper for my business because of my history. I had been a failure at college, had gone to jail, and been deported when I released after two years. First, I needed to build credibility with the public.

As my aunty suggested, I employed the local soccer club to clear the patch behind my aunt's house so I could grow some pumpkins to supplement the pig's feed. I wasted no time. Day in and day out, I was at the pig pen, spending time caressing and patting my pigs. I loved seeing them grow fast so I could send them to the butcher shop even quicker. All the hard work was starting to pay off for me. I owned a few worldly possessions that were beginning to attract people like the bike, the cap, and the RM Williams boots.

Then one Saturday afternoon, something happened. While I was sitting in my pig pen, a boy about seventeen years old suddenly showed up. He was from a nearby village called Bubulu. He hadn't finished his formal schooling, and the man who married his mother left her when he was six months old. He didn't know the man and had never felt the love of a father. The man left his mum because he found out that she was pregnant before he married her. This young man was not blood related to this man and felt that the woman had been unfair to him.

The teenager's name was Joseph Yagayo. He had had a rough upbringing without a father. I knew him to be a pain in the community. Everybody hated him because of his wayward ways. He was a disgrace to his mum.

Joseph had joined a group of boys about the same age, and at night, they would steal chickens and cook them along the river, far away from the owners. They did this on Sundays because everybody was in church. He usually didn't come home until two in the morning. His mother's heart had been broken many times because the boy was heading down the wrong path. She worried that he was a lost cause, prone to violence and a menace to the community.

"What do you want, young man?" I asked.

"My name is Yagayo. I want to change so I can have the things that you have: a mountain bike, a Chicago Bulls cap, and RM Williams boots," he replied.

"How do you know I have those things you mentioned?"

"My mum told me about you. She talked with your aunt at the market two weeks ago. I told my mum I want to have the things that you have, and she said the only way for me to have them is to associate with the person who already has them. That's why I came today to see you. And, to be honest, I'm tired of living the lifestyle of stealing chickens and pigs. I want something new and different," Yagayo said. "I am a member of a group, all teenagers. We are a problem in the community, and I don't want to live that life anymore. It's empty and has no meaning. I want more and am willing to do anything to get out of the muck. The sooner I get out, the better because I want to have the things that I covet."

"Did your friends know that you're here?" I asked.

"No, they don't."

"Have you ever gone to school?"

"It's because of the lack of money in my family, but I only reached grade two. Now, I'm just a village boy, looking for a change, and so I have come to see you. I am willing to do anything to get a step-up in life. I would like to work for you here with the pigs."

"Wow! I'm impressed by your determination to change. Okay, no worries. I'll talk to my aunt tonight. You make sure you get back here tomorrow to hear the outcome of your request," I said to the young boy.

Yagayo went home after meeting with me, feeling ecstatic and hoping for a positive outcome from my aunt and me.

When he arrived home, his mother said, "Where have you been, Yagayo?"

"I've been to Maduku's pigpen, and we chatted. I am looking for change and meaning in my life. I'm tired of the life that I've been living, one without purpose or significance. I want more. I know there is more to life than stealing, even if it is stealing for survival. I asked him to hire me. I want to have the things that you told me he has: the mountain bike, Chicago Bulls cap, and RM Williams boots. Guess what? I've seen the things with my own eyes today. He said he will talk with his aunt tonight, and tell me the outcome tomorrow. So I will go back to see him again."

"That was brave and courageous of you, seeking change and meaning for your life. I never in my wildest dreams thought you would break away from your pack. I'm so proud of you, son, "she said.

I had a chat with my aunt, and she agreed that Yagayo was welcome to come on board. She explained:

When someone suddenly shows uninvited like that, don't turn him down. They are at a pivotal moment in their lives when they need to get their acts together. The universe is calling them to wake up and do something because they are not going to remain young forever. Every single day, week, month, and year that passes, their bodies are growing older, their ages are getting higher, but the years to their deaths are decreasing. It's the sad reality that we all face, and as we grow older every day, we are getting closer to the graveyard.

So Yagayo seeking change, meaning, and a sense of purpose for his life, that's the universe telling him that he needs to wake up and do something with his life before he leaves the planet. Life has its own way of talking to us. Although he initially wanted to work for material possessions, it's more than that. I believe that destiny is calling that boy. Who knows, he might rescue his group members from the lifestyle of stealing that they have been living. He might be the conduit for change for his friends. If he doesn't break out from the pack, how can his friends see the light and realize that they have been living in darkness? So don't hesitate to bring Yagayo on board. We never know what the future holds for people like that, people who personally look for change. They don't need a sermon or to be preached to by an evangelist or someone knocking on their door with a religious pamphlet or brochure.

I was willing to give Yagayo a chance to change by hiring him. The next day, Yagayo checked back in with me, and I was happy to be able to give him good news. "Welcome aboard, Yagayo. My aunt agreed that you should be given an opportunity because you have demonstrated an enormous potential to turn your life. I'm glad to have you come and work with me, doing nothing but feeding pigs. I won't ask you to do something that I never did myself. So are you going to lodge with me, or stay at your mother's house and come to work every day?"

"I reckon it's best to lodge with you, so that I can avoid temptation from my group to fall back and start stealing again. Isolation would be a good thing for me, as I'm vulnerable and might join them again because they are a majority. But I need to talk to my mom first," Yagayo replied.

Yagayo talked to his mother, and she agreed for him to live with me. It consisted of two short trousers and two black tee shirts. He arrived with everything he had in an empty ten-kilogram bag of rice, and he settled into his new life, working on my piggery farm.

My aunt and I made sure he was well-fed and looked after. His mother would often visit on Sundays after church to see how her son was doing. As the weeks and months progressed and he celebrated his first year on the pig farm, Yagayo finally had the desires of his heart come true. He had the mountain bike, the Chicago cap, and the RM Williams boots. In addition, he was a changed man. He abandoned the works of darkness and was heading in a new direction. He had new clothes and a new ukulele that he had taught himself to play. He even composed some songs about working on the piggery farm.

I loved listening to him play after work. He composed a song about a boy who writes a letter to a girl, and he sends that letter to his best friend who is another girl and asks her to deliver it to the girl he loves. Little did he realize that his best friend had feelings for him, too, and she replied to all his letters herself without delivering it to the one they were intended for. He finds out that his best friend is the one who has been replying to his letters. They finally marry each other and have a wonderful marriage because they were already good friends before they fell in love.

He also composed songs about elected officials who failed to deliver on their promises to the people who voted for them. I decided to buy a guitar and play melody to his songs. We became good friends, making music, feeding pigs, and loving what we do.

One Saturday in May during his second year on the pig farm, he rode his mountain bike to the market, wearing his Chicago Bulls cap and the RM Williams boots. He was the center of attention as he walked around buying bananas and pineapples. His former group mates saw him approaching and said, "What's up, man! Long time no see! We heard you were living and working with Maduku or something. Life isn't the same without you around. How did you get the bike, the cap, and the boots? We want the things that you have. Tell us how you got them? Did you steal them from someone or somewhere?"

"I did not steal them," Yagayo said. "I worked and got the money and paid for these things in cash. Besides, I have a new ukulele and am composing and singing songs with my boss on the farm. This is my second year now, working with him, feeding, breeding, and selling pigs."

"Wow! At least you do something worthwhile with your time, dude, not like us. What we do gives us no return for our time and effort. Stealing just isn't worth it," said Kekara Manepo, one of the boys. "Ask your boss if he has any jobs for us. We want to work, and we're tired of living this lifestyle. We wanted meaning and substance in our lives. You are an inspiration to all of us because you have what most teenagers our age wish to have in their lives."

"I will talk with him tonight. We are expanding the operation and probably need some extra hands. I'll let you what he thinks," Yagayo said.

Kekara Manepo and his boys walked back to Bubulu village with great anticipation, talking about how they would feel if they got a chance to work. They discussed the attention they would get for obtaining the material possessions Maduku and Yagayo possessed. They were excited and couldn't wait to hear what Maduku would say and hoping the response would be a positive one. The desire to have the things Yagayo had burned like fire in their bones.

Yagayo got home and told me that he had bumped into his old friends at the market. "Guess what? I stumbled across my friends at the market today. They were so excited to see me again. They were fascinated by the things I own: the mountain bike, the Chicago Bulls cap, and the RM Williams boots. They thought I stole them from somewhere, but I told them I worked for these things. They want to have these things in their lives, too, but they don't know how to get them. One of them—his name is Kekara Manepo—actually rode my mountain bike, and he loved it. They touched the bike and my cap. They also looked at how shiny my boots were. They were intrigued. They asked me how I obtained these things, and I told them that I worked for these things, and I didn't steal them. They wanted me to ask you if you have a job for them. They are tired of living the lifestyle of stealing and inflicting pain in the community. They want change, to get out, but don't know how to salvage themselves from the situation they are trapped in," Yagayo said. "The look in their eyes tells you that they are desperate for change. They are hopeless and lost, barely making it in life."

"Aunty, did you hear what Yagayo just said?" I said, turning to her. "His old friends want change and are looking for meaning in their lives. They asked him if I might have a job for them. We are expanding at the moment, and might need to hire some people."

"How many of them wanted a job?" Rose Mary asked.

"Four people," Yagayo said.

"Get them on board, but first, we need to establish some common understanding with their parents. We need to let them know why their kids want to work on the piggery farm. We don't want people to blame us if their kids' expectations are met with disappointment. However, what we can guarantee is that with hard work, perseverance, and self-discipline, anything is possible. Tomorrow after work, you ride to the village to inform them that we need to talk with their parents first. Maduku will write four little notes to give to each of the boys' parents, letting them know of their kids' desperation to come and work on the piggery farm," Rose Mary said.

I wrote the little notes and handed them to Yagayo. He quickly rode to the village that he was born and raised in. He delivered the notes to the parents of his four friends. After reading the notes, the parents were surprised to know what their kids wanted to do with their lives, but they wanted to know if this was a plan that would work for their boys. After talking with Yagayo, they remembered that he had been living the same way as their children had, and they knew that if it had worked for Yagayo, it could work for the boys, too. They believed in the power of association as a vehicle for change.

The parents all came to my village to sit down and talk with me and my aunt. They wanted confirmation that their kids' desire for change and for work had been explained to me. After some discussion, it was agreed that the boys would come to work with Yagayo and me. Yagayo was also present at the meeting, dressed in black from head to toe. The parents' doubts were addressed, and a common understanding was reached. The boys moved in to stay with Yagayo and work on the piggery farm. My life experiences spoke louder to them than my words. Yagayo's friends finally left behind their works of hatred and pain, and joined Yagayo on the road to change, prosperity, and freedom to live life on one's own terms.

My team and I had the tremendous responsibility to look after more than three hundred pigs. We had sales coming in from weddings, the christening of newborn babies, church commemorations, birthday parties, the ordination of priests and lay workers to oversee certain positions in the church, and from soccer clubs who had won a trophy from tournaments in the region. Yagayo's four friends knew that he and I had too much money in the bank.

As the weeks and the months progressed, the new recruits joined the team. They were doing well, and in the third year, we had more than five hundred pigs. I now realized that one of his problems—the lack of money—was finally solved. At this point in time, I was making too much money. I was feeling good about creating more and more money. It was exciting. But now I knew I had to use the money to support and accommodate the second problem: illiteracy. Illiteracy was the main reason that most people didn't reach their potential. It was what isolated them and kept them from connecting with people from diverse backgrounds and cultures on the island and abroad.

One beautiful Monday morning, Yagayo and I went into town to deposit money in our personal and business accounts. We caught the eyes of two beautiful women, working as bank tellers at the bank. They were amazed at the amount of money we were depositing, especially since we were so young people. They were curious and wanted to know if we had studied business and finance at college. The amount of money we were depositing was greater than what we had initially opened our accounts with. Their names were Ms. Grace Masisimia and Ms. Mercy Masatola. They were single and working in the bank.

Grace and Mercy were nearly inseparable. They had lunch together every day, and hit the market on Saturdays, looking at jewelry and knitted and sewn woollen baskets bearing the colors of the rainbow. The only thing missing in their lives was that special someone. Otherwise, these two girls were equipped and ready to settle down and navigate life with its challenges, always moving forward.

One of them, Ms. Masisimia, bravely asked out of curiosity, "Hey gentlemen, I'm just wondering where you two got the money in your accounts? I know you've been our clients for over two years now, but what you've deposited today far exceeds what you originally opened the accounts with! It's quite interesting for young people your age to have that kind of money in just two years! I've been working here for almost eight years now as a bank teller, and I have never come across people your age earning the amount of money you deposited today.

"It's not a big deal, but I'm just curious and would love to know. You know, I might tender my resignation to the bank and come work for you guys handling the financial aspects your business, if you own a company or something!" Ms. Masisimia said. Her workmate, Mercy, was listening from her cubicle. They had both graduated from college with diplomas in business and finance.

"We are actually from the village. We are pig farmers. That's what we do, and that's what we love doing. That's where all the money in the accounts came from. I am the founder, and I have five boys working with me, including Yagayo. We are six altogether. They are just school dropouts, kicked out by the system. I just gave them a little help to get them started," I said.

"As the founder, did you study business at a college? What is your educational background?" Grace asked.

"I managed to get a scholarship to study Human Resource management at a college overseas, but I didn't finish. As a matter of fact, I was so stupid that I went to jail and was deported out of the country when I was released," I said.

"Oh, that's unfortunate. What happened, if you don't mind telling me?" Grace continued her investigation.

"Girl trouble," I said laughing. "I was a fool to fall for her juicy words, her beauty, and her charm. I don't blame her, though. It's all my fault," I said.

"That's sad to hear. So are you seeing someone after that mess?" Grace asked.

"No, I'm not. But for now, I'm managing to keep it all together. I'm in no hurry to date again, but I remain open if the opportunity presents itself. I don't want to spend precious time looking for it. Instead, I spend time developing myself to be an asset, so that when I give myself to someone, I am giving something valuable that is going to enhance and add value to their lives, you know," I explained.

"I admire your philosophy for living," Grace said.

"What about you? Do you have a family of your own, kids or something?" I asked her.

She hesitated. "I am involved at the moment, but I'm still unsure of where it is going. I have received and endured horrible verbal abuse and treatment that has hurt me emotionally. I need to slow down and allow the dust to settle. It's all a bit cloudy at the moment. He is studying at university on a scholarship, but he lacks direction and has no vision for himself. Anyway, nice talking to you. hope to see you on your next visit."

We walked out of the bank, and Grace walked over to Mercy's cubicle. "Did you hear the questions I was asking those two gentlemen?"

"Yes, I did," Mercy said.

"Weren't they handsome and adorable young men?" Grace sighed.

"What do you mean? You mean your heart is reacting to one of them? Which one?" Mercy asked.

"I admired the founder, Mr. Maduku. The way he talks is both engaging and intellectually stimulating," Grace said.

"I could tell that when you were talking to him. My heart was beating and pounding fast. I know life has more to offer than we are receiving now. The guys we are dating are just hopeless. They're abusive, disrespectful, and always asking for money."

"I don't know what they do with their student allowances," Mercy said. "I am putting all options on the table now, whether to continue dating him or not. I know I have so much to offer, and I can't just settle for anyone. I have come too long a way to settle for crumbs."

"So how are you going to express your feelings to him?" Mercy asked.

"I will formally write to him, and give him the note on his next visit," Grace said.

"Awesome! Expressing your feelings toward someone in a handwritten manner means that time, effort, and consideration have been a deep part of writing the letter. What about the other guy who came with him? Is he single or involved?" Mercy asked.

"You mean Mr. Yagayo? I guess he is single like his boss because there was no ring on his finger. Maduku mentioned that all the boys working with him are single, including him."

"Having too much money tucked away in the bank and remaining single is incomprehensible. What's wrong with all the girls in his neighborhood? It's unfathomable," Mercy said.

"You only know the answer if you ask. Asking is the hallmark of curiosity. When you ask the right questions, you get the right answers. It saves time and energy," Grace said.

"I agree. If so, go ahead and write that letter girl. I will follow in your footsteps. We can write letters to the guys at university calling it quits if we change course and direction," Mercy said.

After work, Grace went home and jotted down her feelings in her writing pad, using a black ballpoint pen. She felt calm and serene about it and knew it was the right thing to do. The timing was right. She was going to write two letters: one to Maduku, and one to Samson Galorodo, the man she had been dating.

After she wrote the one to give to Maduku, she wrote the one to post to Samson. In her letter to Mr. Galorodo, she said she needed a break, she needed some space, and she needed some time to deal with some issues in her personal life, issues that might deny and rob her of becoming the ideal woman she was meant to be in a man's life. She said needed to deal with issues such as low self-esteem, self-doubt, and insecurities about her body image. She told Samson that she needed to slow down and conduct a self-examination of how far she had traveled in life, and the adjustments and changes she needed to make for the future. She needed some time to think and didn't want to rush into something she wasn't ready for, spending precious time later to deal with regrets instead of growing and enjoying life in its abundance with the one she loves. She addressed a letter to Maduku and one to Samson. She posted Samson's letter at the post office but held on to Maduku's to give to him in person.

Two weeks later, Yagayo and I went into town again to deposit some more money. "Hello, Mr. Maduku and Mr. Yagayo, how are you two doing?" Grace greeted us warmly.

"We are doing well, thank you." I said.

"How can I help?" she asked.

"We would like to deposit some money into the accounts," Yagayo said.

"Not a problem, I can help you do that. How is the piggery farm? And the boys?" She asked while counting the notes.

"Not bad at all. So far, so good," I said. "They are happy. We made a few sales the other day so they have some money coming in. We killed two pigs and had a small party so I could show my appreciation for what they've been doing since they joined my team. We invited the whole village to join us. We keep expanding to accommodate the new piglets born these past few weeks and months. We also started a pumpkin farm to supplement our mill run. When we are done here, we will go to the local supplier to get some more mill run. On our next visit, we might bring the boys to open passbook savings account with the bank. For now, they just keep their money under their pillows in a plastic bag."

"That is a very good idea," Grace said.

"I told them how important it is to save money. I said saving money gives you stability and peace of mind. It gives you leverage to handle and manage tough times. That is one of the things I taught them based on my personal experience in dealing with money," I said. "I taught them that it is not how much you earn that matters, but it is how much you keep that matters."

"That's excellent money advice! I didn't learn that in my business studies at college. I learned about big concepts and theories but never about what you taught your boys," Grace said. "Anyway, here is a note for you, for your eyes only. Have a read and get back to me in writing with your response."

I put the envelope in my backpack. Yagayo and I left the bank and went to the mill run supplier. We bought fifteen bags of fish meal and mill run, and at three o'clock in the afternoon, we boarded the yellow Mazda truck to go home.

"That was so brave of you to hand a letter to someone in person like that. How are you feeling now?" Mercy asked Grace.

"Well, we are adults. I feel good because if you want something, say it or do it. Don't just think about it without taking any action. Don't allow the fear of rejection to hold you back. You never know unless you try, and I'm expressing myself and making myself vulnerable in that letter."

"I admire your courageous attitude. I will write to Yagayo after we hear the response to your application from Maduku. I think I need to say goodbye to Mr. Ahimaaz Soekeni and move on, too. And I need you to help me write the letter," Mercy said.

"Of course, I'll do that for you because you are my sister and my best friend," Grace said.

When I got home, I read the letter and showed it to my aunt. I told her that this woman had caught my eye the very first time I had visited the bank to open the accounts, but I was too shy to express it in writing then. "Look at what Grace, the lady at the bank, gave me today," I exclaimed.

"Did she really give this to you in person? If she works at the bank, she is a college graduate with a diploma in business and finance. But you are not. You didn't finish college like her. Her family might have high expectations for her. They probably want her to marry someone at her level, someone with a college qualification. I have heard stories about where she comes from.

Girls from her region, their parents always want them to marry well-educated men, at least someone with a college diploma or degree. That is my only fear for you. But I don't want to discourage and frighten you. Write back to her and explain your humble background and your reservation about not being in the same class as her. Tell her you might disappoint her parents," my aunt said. "And not only that, but you need to know if you are ready for the commitment and responsibility that comes with marriage. You have been through so much and need to know that you are healed and ready to commit until your dying day because marriage is not a joke. Marriage is not for life; marriage is for death. Only death has the absolute right to separate any matrimonial covenant."

I wrote the letter, explaining my reservation and nervousness to Grace's application. In my reply, I advised her to consult with her parents first to gain their approval or find out if they only want her marrying someone with a college diploma. I told her to talk with her parents to reach a consensus, and get back to me in writing, hopefully with their consent. I stated that it was vitally important for her to preserve and protect the close-knit relationship with her family.

I didn't have time to go into town to deliver the letter so I sent it by the driver of the yellow Mazda truck. I asked him to deliver the letter to the bank to Ms. Grace Masisimia.

Grace received Maduku's letter of reservation and nervousness. She read it carefully and understood where he was coming from. Personally, she didn't care whether Maduku was a college graduate or not. All she cared about was marrying someone who had her best interests at heart, and someone who knew where he is going so he could take her and their children to that place of adventure and happiness.

She consulted her parents and told them about Maduku, the piggery farmer and a client of her bank. She told them she had very strong feelings for him, that he seemed like he was going somewhere, and she wanted to go there with him and her future kids. Her parents respected and honored her decision to drop Samson Galorodo and start something serious and meaningful with Maduku.

"As long as you are happy, we are fine with that. At the end of the day, you—not us—are responsible for your ultimate happiness. You are responsible for the outcome of the choices you make. As your parents, we do not have any objections about you marrying a piggery farmer. Already, his background speaks for itself, and you have decided to marry and live with him and support what he is doing," her father said. "One thing that we ask of you is to meet this man that you admire and love. We want to have lunch with him at a restaurant in town, so I can talk with him. Let's book next weekend to give him ample time to adjust his plans for that day."

"No worries, I'll write him a letter so he can organize and make adjustments to any plans he might have on that date," Grace said.

She wrote back to Maduku, including in her reply the consent and approval of her parents for her to go on a date with him and their request to meet him in person at a restaurant in town. She gave the letter to the driver of the yellow Mazda truck to deliver it to Maduku's village. She also gave the driver a box of clothes for his wife and kids. The driver was thrilled to know someone from the bank because it would be helpful if he wanted to loan money from the bank to buy a new truck.

He drove the letter to my village and offered to take my reply back to Grace at the bank. "I can bring your reply to Grace Masisimia if you want. Just wait beside the road to hand it to me when I pass through. This will save you money and time," he said.

"Thank you very much. Sending the letter with you is much quicker and cheaper, and it reaches the recipient's hands in a matter of hours," I said.

I'm happy to do it," he replied.

I read Grace's letter and was thrilled to have the approval and consent of her parents for us to start. I accepted her application and was relieved and hopeful that Grace had looked beyond my educational background and wanted to marry me. I replied to Grace's letter in writing and gave it to the driver of the yellow truck to deliver.

Finally, the day to meet Grace's parents arrived. I delegated some of the daily tasks to the boys and went to town to meet them for lunch. I traveled with the driver of the yellow truck, sitting in the front seat. The other passengers were wondering why I was sitting with the driver in the front seat. Little did they know the driver was laying the groundwork for the future. He knew that something bigger and better would come out of his relationship with Grace and me. He had been the mail carrier for their exchange of letters.

It was Saturday, and the small town was buzzing with people running errands and shopping at the shops. The driver dropped me off in front of the bank, and there was Grace with her parents waiting for me.

"That's him, Daddy, the one in black from head to toe," Grace said to her father. I walked towards them and was greeted by her father.

"Hello, son. I am Mr. Paul Masisimia, Grace's father, and you are Mr. Maduku Mamata, right?" he said.

"Yes, I am the one." I shook hands with Grace and greeted my future mother-in-law with a hug and a kiss.

We walked to Auki restaurant and ordered some lunch. I chose Chicken Schnitzel and chips. I was sitting next to Grace's mother, and Grace was sitting next to her father across the table. While we were eating, Mr. Masisimia asked me some questions regarding my vision for living and my opinion about marriage and what it meant to me.

"Yes, Maduku, Grace mentioned to me and her mother that she's interested in you. She told us that you are the ideal man, and she wants to spend the rest of her life with you and grow old gracefully. We respect her choice, and we asked her if we could meet with you in person. Tell me about you and your vision for your life?"

"First, I would like to thank you for lunch and the opportunity for us to come together so you could meet me. In brief, I want to build a school and establish businesses to create employment at home in order to control urban drift and migration to distant shores. I am a pig farmer. That's what I do for a living. I'm pretty sure Grace told you that already. I want to use the pig as the mechanism, the vehicle, the platform on which to stand and reach out into other areas. When I say other areas, I mean other business opportunities that are economical and environmentally friendly to nature, not destructive. In the words of scripture, nothing is new under the sun. All that is left is the discovery part of it. I have all of this written down in black and white. Remember, a vision is not a vision until it is documented. So I had my life's plan and vision written down. I had one for business, one for my family, one for my future kids, one for me and my future wife, and one for my community." When I mentioned I had a vision for my wife, everybody smiled, including Grace.

"What is the vision for your community?" Mr. Masisimia asked.

"Well, first, we need to identify what makes up a community. A community is comprised of family units, and family units consist of a husband, wife, and kids. The head of a family is the father. He is the authority in the home. Hence, if we want a strong community, we must empower the fathers because they shoulder the weight of the family unit. They are the foundation of the house, upon which the whole structure stands. When the father is empowered, we will have a strong family, a strong community, and eventually a strong nation, because a nation is comprised of communities.

"To answer your question of my vision for my community, that is how I want to go about executing it: training and empowering the fathers to discover their authority and position in the family. When we have strong fathers, we have a strong nation," I said.

"I have never heard it put like that. I think you really do have a vision. In fact, you are a visionary, no doubt about it. You really know where you are going. Grace, I think you made the right choice and it's a good one. Welcome into the family, Maduku," Mr. Masisimia said with a firm handshake across the table. "It's great to meet you. I think while we are here, we need to seal this meeting with the engagement ring. Do you have a ring on your finger?" he asked me.

"Yes I do."

"Alright, put that on Grace's finger as a sign that she is engaged. I will tell my people that Grace is now an engaged woman so that there is no tension or ill-feelings when they see you two walking around in town," Mr. Masisimia said.

The engagement ring was placed on Grace's finger, and I, too, had one on my finger. We officially began dating after that meeting.

While we were getting to know and learn more about each other, we mapped out our plans for the future we wanted to create. Grace received a reply to her letter from Samson Galorodo at the university. He accused her of making excuses about needing time and space for self-reflection and examination when she was actually seeing someone else and intend-ed to move on. He was angry and threatened to hurt Grace, me, and the kids if he saw us in town. Those were his threats, but, in the same letter, he promised to change his behavior if Grace was patient and gave him one more chance and didn't give up on him. He tried to convince her that people can change. Grace didn't bother to reply. She was done with Samson. When a girl is done, she is done. Period.

After graduating from college, Grace had experienced and endured much verbal abuse from Samson. He insulted her and asked her for mon-ey to buy alcohol all the time. When he was intoxicated, Grace had to leave her cubicle and hide at the back of the conference room because Samson would go into the bank and ask her for money in front of her col-leagues and clients. He was an embarrassment and a pain. Grace chucked his letter in the trash after reading it and showing it to me.

"He is the same person he was before he went to university. He has just physically relocated," I said to Grace.

While we were spending time together, talking about how many kids we wanted, when to have them, where we wanted to live, and where we wanted to visit, Grace asks me about my apprentice, Mr. Joseph Yagayo. She wanted to know if he was single.

"Hey, Maduku, I'm just wondering about your apprentice, Mr. Yagayo. Is he single or not?"

"Why are you asking?" I said.

"My workmate, Ms. Mercy Masatola, she is like me, too, dating someone toxic and abusive like Samson Galorodo. He is studying at a university like Samson but in a different country. She wants to get out of that relationship. Her boyfriend rings up every single day, asking her for money. I remember one time, he rang and verbally abused her on the phone, telling her that she was low class, damned and stupid, just worked in the bank, was useless and had never gone to a university like him. Mercy cried and hung up the phone.

She had to go home early, and she didn't come to work for a week. She was hurt and badly bruised by those insulting comments he had thrown at her on the phone. I don't know why it's so hard to find a good man, men who know where they are going in life like you. You know, a man with a vision is necessary and attractive to a woman. Women love visionary men. There is no point in having material possessions or tons of money in the bank or a tertiary qualification if you don't know where you are going!" Grace said. "After you have those things, you realize they have no emotions or feelings. We are emotional beings. You can't relate to material possessions. Money comes from a tree. You can't relate to a tree. It has no emotions and feelings.

Money is like a chisel, a circular saw, or a hammer. You use it to get work done. After using it, you tuck it away in a cupboard or in a toolbox for future use. That is all there is to it. And a tertiary qualification? You laminate it, put it in a frame, hang it on the wall, or put it in a suitcase. That's all there is to it! Nothing more, nothing less. Instead, it is the precious times spent together, interacting with people, and getting involved and engaged in activities for the good of the community and its people. That is what gives meaning and makes life worth living. The social contribution we give to making people's lives better is what provides ultimate satisfaction and fulfillment. One's personal contribution is like an apple tree, serving its fruits to its pickers and eaters without expecting gratitude or appreciation in return. It doesn't hurt because you were designed to serve without expectation. It is we, the people, that give money and things meaning. The money and the things themselves have no emotion whatsoever," Grace said.

"You sound convincing and insightful. I'm impressed," said Maduku. "So you telling me that Mr. Yagayo was attracted to Mercy. Is that what you are trying to say?"

"Absolutely correct!"

"Well, it wasn't hard for you. Tell Mercy to write a letter like you did. Tell her to be proactive about making her feelings known in writing. When ordinary people from the village like us see people who work at a bank, we hold them in high esteem, and we are often nervous to talk to them or strike up a conversation with them on the street. The way they dress frightens us because they look so grand, unless they are a relation or a friend or you both have some history, like going to the same primary or high school. Otherwise, we are all strangers on the street. Mr. Yagayo was a school dropout. He didn't finish his primary education. So expecting Yagayo to approach Mercy in person or be the first to write a letter is daunting and not going to happen anytime soon," I said.

"Mercy, too, is having difficulty with writing a letter, so I'll help her and give it to you to deliver to Mr. Yagayo. How does that sound?" Grace asked.

"Sounds awesome."

At work, Grace told Mercy that she had spoken to me about her heart's reaction towards Yagayo, and that my advice for her was to make an informal expression of her feelings in writing.

"Mercy, I've spoken to Maduku about your interest in finding out whether he's involved or not. Maduku has confirmed that Yagayo is single and looking for someone to share his life with. Maduku suggested that you express your feelings in writing like I did. You write the letter yourself first, and then I'll edit and add some flavor and juicy words. You sign it and then we'll send it with the driver of the yellow truck. What do you think?"

"Sounds awesome, Grace!" Mercy said.

Mercy wrote the letter, expressing her feelings, desires, and her first impression of Mr. Yagayo at the bank. She made it clear from the outset that she didn't want someone just because he had a college certificate, diploma, or degree. All she wants is someone who can give her attention, affection, and appreciation, and bring out the best in her. Someone who could cultivate a conducive environment for her to grow in and blossom like a flower, and not feel threatened or intimidated by a woman who is successful. She finished the letter and gave it to Grace to read. Grace was surprised that Mercy could say so much and be so honest about her thoughts and feelings in three short paragraphs. She made a few minor corrections and gave it back to Mercy to sign. After she signed the letter, Grace gave it to the driver to deliver to Yagayo. Grace wanted the best for Mercy. She wanted to see her smiling and happy.

Yagayo received Mercy's letter and was confused. He showed me the letter and asked me to read it to him. He had only finished a grade two education and couldn't even apply what he had learned at that level.

"Hey, Maduku, here is a letter. I don't know where it comes from. Could you please read it to me?"

"Of course." I tore open the envelope and read the letter to him. After I finished, I laughed and shook Yagayo's hands. "Congratulations, buddy! Someone admires and adores you. You remember the lady at the bank, sitting next to the one who assisted us with opening our bank accounts?"

"Yes, I do."

"She's the one who wrote this letter to you. She likes you, man!"

Yagayo was astonished. "Who am I? I am Yagayo, and I finished second-grade. I can barely read at all, and can't even spell or write my own name. I work on a farm. What does she adore or admire about me? This is ridiculous, unreal. She is a college graduate and works at a financial institution. I am not in the same class as her. Girls like that, their parents have high expectations for them, and want them to marry someone with a college diploma or degree," Yagayo said.

"Listen, Yagayo, she stated in this letter that she wasn't looking for a college graduate or someone with a lot of money. All she wants and looks for in a man is attention, appreciation, and affection. These are the three things a woman needs. Money, houses, cars, and expensive apparel mean nothing to a woman if she is not receiving these three things from her man on a daily basis," I said, encouragingly.

"Well, you are my boss. What is your assessment of me? Do you think I'm ready?" Yagayo asked.

"Yes, I think you are ready. You are independent, and you are working. If you are independent and can look after yourself, then you are ready to look after someone coming into your life. I think you possess those things—the three A's—that Mercy is looking for in a man. Besides, you have too much money already in the bank.

"Building a house for her and giving her the things she might need in the house is not a problem at all. You can follow her in town and pay for whatever she needs to make her home beautiful. The furniture, bedding, cooking utensils, and so forth. It's her house, so don't worry about buying anything for the house without her approval. She might arrive and disagree with you. Leave that to her, and you just be ready to pay for everything," I explained.

"Alright, no worries. Write the reply, and say that her application is successful. If she is looking for a man who can give her attention, affection, and appreciation, then she has found the ideal and suitable man for the job," Yagayo said. I constructed Yagayo's reply and handed it to the driver to deliver.

When she received the reply from Yagayo, Mercy was thrilled to have found the right man who could meet her emotional needs. She loved Yagayo for the person he was, not for his money he had in the bank. She knew that together, they could make money to put in the hands of those who had a vision and a plan to achieve their dreams. She told her parents about Yagayo. Her parents had no objection to Mercy's adoration of Yagayo, but wanted to see what kind of man he was, the man who had won their daughter's heart. They knew how much Mercy had already been through.

"Listen, sweetheart, your mother and I want to meet that man first. As parents, we don't want to see you hurt time and time again, like the verbal abuse you've been getting from Ahimaaz Soekeni," her father said. "We want the man you marry to treat you with respect and dignity, not as a sex object and machine for producing babies. You are a human first! Equal in status, value, and contribution."

"Okay, I will write Yagayo a letter and organize the meeting." Mercy, like Grace, booked the Saturday of the following week for the meeting.

At work, Grace asked Mercy about her meeting with her parents. "How is it going, darling?" she said.

"It's awesome. My parents want to meet Yagayo in person," she said.

"Same process as mine," Grace said. "Parents always have their kid's best interest at heart. They want their kids to be happy in marriage and in life." "So we are going to write two letters?" Mercy said. "A goodbye one for Ahimaaz Soekeni and one for Yagayo? Just write one for Yagayo. For Ahimaaz, I want to ring him and tell him that I'm done with him. I don't want to correspond or keep him in suspense. I want him to hear it from me that it's over, that I'm done.

Grace constructed Mercy's reply to Yagayo, informing him that her parents wanted to meet him, and she booked Saturday of the following week for the meeting. Mercy took the letter and gave it to the driver. The driver was now the mail carrier for these girls in their letter exchanges with Maduku and Yagayo. It was quicker and cheaper. The mail was in the addressee's hands within 24 hours of despatch.

Yagayo received the letter from Mercy and gave it to me to read it to him. He was excited and noted the date for the meeting. He asked me for advice on how to address Mercy's father and give him a brief description of his vision for his life.

Grace was twenty-eight years old, and Mercy was twenty-five. So Grace took the lead in matters pertaining to letter writing and courtship, and advised Mercy. They had gone to college together, graduated together, worked at the same bank, and now they had reached the pivotal moment of choosing a partner for life. They want their partners to be good to them, which would be different from the past.

After work, I told my aunt that Mercy had expressed interest in Yagayo, and that she had actually written a letter to make known her feelings toward him. "I read the letter to Yagayo and explained the contents of the letter. He was sold on Mercy's proposal."

"That's interesting," my aunt said. "You boys certainly got the girls attention. That didn't happen in my generation. Usually, it was the men who pursued the ladies. But I think if you want something so badly, you better make some moves and hope for the best. I am happy for you boys," Rose Mary said.

"I replied to Mercy's application on Yagayo's behalf, stating his reservation to date her because he is not well-educated or a college graduate like her. Mercy wrote back that she was not looking for any of the excuses that Yagayo might have in his mind. She said all she cares about is someone who can give her attention, affection, and appreciation. That is all she is looking for in a man," I explained to my aunt.

"Mercy is absolutely right! All the material things that men want to impress women with are secondary and bear little significance. Those things themselves have no warmth and touch," she said.

"Mercy eventually booked a date for Yagayo to meet her parents on

Saturday, next week. I did a little coaching session with Yagayo on how to behave and present himself to Mercy's father. When Yagayo comes back from meeting with her parents, I would like to take the four boys into town to open a savings account with the bank. Progressive accounts would suit them best for investing," I said.

"That's awesome. It's best to start saving early in life. Those are good things, Maduku. If something seems good to you and you want the same for others, do it. After all, they have left family and friends to work with you. They believe that life can be a little better than where they were," Rose Mary said.

Saturday arrived, and it was a big day for Yagayo. He boarded the yellow truck to meet with Mercy's parents. There were many passengers going into town, some to sell their produce, some to board the ship to travel to the capital city. They picked up some passengers along the road and got into the little town around 9:00 a.m. Mercy and her parents were waiting for Yagayo to arrive. The truck stopped in front of the bank, one of the main stops right in the heart of town. Yagayo paid for his truck fare and greeted Mercy with a handshake. She introduced him to her parents.

"Hello, I'm Yagayo, nice to meet you," he said nervously.

"Hello, Yagayo, nice to meet you," her father said.

"Hello, I'm Mercy's mother." Yagayo shook her hand.

"Let's go and sit by the sea. We need to buy cassava pudding and fish and some green coconuts at the market," Mercy's father said.

"That's a good idea. I'll pay for the groceries," Mercy said.

"Thank you, my sweet daughter, I appreciate that," her father said.

As they sat by the sea, facing the ocean and enjoying their food, Mercy's father asked Yagayo if he was serious about marrying his daughter. "Mercy told me and her mother that she loved you so much and you loved her. Is that true?"

"Actually, I was minding my own business, working on the farm feeding pigs when I got this letter delivered by a driver from the village I'm living in. I have a grade two education and can't even spell my own name, let alone read. I gave the letter to my boss to read it for me. I was shocked when he said a lady working at the bank had a crush on me. I had seen Mercy at the bank when my boss and I opened a savings account, but I was too shy to approach her because she was so high above me, academically speaking. My boss asked me if I remembered the beautiful lady sitting in the next cubicle beside the teller who was serving us at that time, and I said yes. He said, 'Well, she has a crush on you, and she has expressed her feelings for you in this letter.'

When I heard that I responded, 'Who am I? I'm just an ordinary bloke with no status of any sort. I'm from the village, never went past second-grade education, feed pigs to make a living, and never in my wildest dreams thought a beautiful lady with such class would have a crush on me. My boss replied on my behalf, stating very clearly my reservations about Mercy's letter. She replied and took it another notch further, saying that she wasn't looking for someone educated or a college graduate with prestigious credentials. All she ever wants from a man is attention, affection, and appreciation. Everything else is secondary. I was sold straight away because that's exactly what kind of person I am. I possess those traits and qualities," Yagayo said.

"That's interesting to know. So what are your dreams and hopes for the future?" Mercy's father asked.

"My dreams and hopes for the future are to be a better man, a better husband to my future wife, and a good father to my future kids. I want to be a successful businessman so I can effectively contribute to the development in my community and beyond. I want to provide power to the people using swine manure. I don't know how to do that right now, but the thought is always on my mind. I might need to do some research and get an engineer to sketch my thoughts onto a piece of paper. At the moment, I am saving money and living below my means, living in the village," Yagayo said.

"Well, Mercy has gone through so much pain in her previous relationship. We respect her choice and want her to be happy. We trust that you will look after her and help bring out the best in her. We trust that you will provide the warmth and comfort she needs when it's cold and lonely, when the moon refuses to shine and there is no sunshine in her world after the rain. We trust that you will strive to make her happiness your ultimate priority and responsibility in your life," Mercy's father said.

"I don't promise that I'm the ideal man because I am still a work in progress, still growing and learning. I think the most important thing is communication. We must communicate to iron out any misunderstandings between us in our marriage. When we talk about issues, we will have the clarification and the answers we are seeking to maintain peace and harmony in the family," Yagayo said.

"We are glad to give you our daughter. We know that there is no perfect marriage in the world. I liken marriage to a rose flower. A rose plant has thorns. If you love the roses, you have to love and embrace the thorns as well. You cannot have the roses without the thorns. It's impossible because they are inseparable. Having that understanding will breed patience and tolerance in a marriage covenant.

"Moreover, to have a wonderful marriage, I liken it to a fire, another analogy that I love so much. In order for the fire to keep burning, one must keep putting in the right piece of wood. Otherwise, the flame dies out, and all you are left with is smoke. And you will suffocate. Many beautiful marriages die out because couples were ignorant of the right piece of wood to put on the fire to keep it burning. I trust that you have learned and mastered the three most important pieces of wood to put on the fire: attention, affection, and appreciation.

"When you apply these three on a daily basis, your wife will give you the stars, the moon, the world, and everything in it. When you make her feel like she's not an option but your priority, you don't need to beg or fight for her to take you for a ride down south around the island and the neighborhood. We will arrange a time to hold an evening tea for the engagement," her father said. "Sweetheart, is there anything you want to say or add?" he asked his wife. "I like Yagayo. He is a fine gentleman. He is ready because he has a job and is working. They are both working so they are ready to give and share with each other," Mercy's mother said.

"Alright, we are done. Mercy will let you know the date for the engagement, Yagayo. Thanks for coming," her father said shaking his hand.

Yagayo returned home after meeting with Mercy's parents. When he arrived back in the village, I asked him to give me an update. "How's it going, buddy?" I said.

"Mercy's father was impressed. He welcomed me into his family, and he liked my vision for my life. He was sold on the vision I shared."

"That's awesome! I'm excited for you. Now on Monday, we'll take the boys to open their saving accounts with the bank."

We took the four boys to open savings accounts with the bank. The boys had been keeping all their money under their pillows. They all agreed to open their accounts with the same amount of money, six thousand dollars. They boarded the truck on Monday morning and arrived in the little town. I walked to the post office to send a letter to Ms. Nofu Atkins. The boys followed me, and after posting the letter, we walked to the bank.

The boys and I waited in the queue, even though I had connections in the bank. Even though Grace was a teller at the bank, we were required to stand in the queue like everybody else. There was no special treatment here.

Our turn came, and the four boys and I stood in front of Mercy's desk because Grace was serving a female client.

"How can I help you, Maduku?" Mercy said with a smile.

"I want my boys to open savings accounts with the bank."

"Not a problem. I'll help you do that. Who's first?" she asked.

"Mr. Kingston Papaya is first," I said. Mercy filled out all the particulars for Mr. Papaya.

"How much money you want to put in the account?" she asked Kingston.

"Six thousand dollars, please," Papaya said. Mercy's amazement showed in her face. She counted all the notes and put them in the drawer.

"Perfect, now sign here on this dotted line, please. Every time you come to make a deposit, don't forget to bring this passbook with you. Keep this in a dry and safe place," Mercy said to Mr. Papaya. "Who's next?"

"Isaiah Paraka," I said. Mercy followed the same procedure she had done with Kingston.

"How much did you want to put in?"

"Six thousand dollars please," Isaiah said. Mercy wrote down the amount in words. She couldn't believe that the young men had this much money, living in the village and never having been to college or even finished primary education.

"Sign here please," she said.

Paraka signed, and Mercy counted the money. She bundled it and slipped it in the drawer. "Next please."

"Come on, Malachi Kakake. Your turn," I said with a smile. Again this young man had six thousand dollars to deposit.

"Thank you," Malachi said.

"Awesome," Mercy said. She once more counted all the notes and wrote down the amount in words. "Sign here please, where it says signature on the dotted line."

Malachi signed and put his passbook in his pocket.

"And the fourth and the last one," Mercy said, smiling.

"Walter Kiku, your turn," I said. Walter stepped forward.

Mercy again deposited six thousand dollars. Mercy counted the notes just to make sure. "Perfect," she said. "Sign here please, and we're done."

Walter signed his name, and Mercy handed him his new passbook account. "Thank you very much, Mercy," I said.

"It's my great pleasure," Mercy said.

When the boys and I walked out of the bank, Mercy have a deep sigh. She had twenty-four thousand dollars in the cash drawer. "I thought I had seen it all, but I was wrong. Those boys from the village prove that you don't need to go to college to make tons of money. What they earn, for their age, is just unbelievable," she said to Grace.

Grace giggled and said, "I knew that when Maduku mentioned he wanted his boys to open savings accounts with the bank, it was going to be a surprise. They have too much money," Grace said. "I saw that with Maduku and Yagayo. That's the power of teamwork. Everybody wins. I believe we haven't seen anything yet. We are up for a great adventure and more surprises with these boys in the months and years ahead. It is a reflection of what kind of a leader Maduku is. He knows the power of teamwork, and he wants the best for his workers. When his workers succeed, he succeeds. When people see his workers, they see him. The workers portray his image in the public eye. It is a reflection of his leadership. And the speed they are traveling at right now, there is no stopping them. They are invincible."

As time progressed, Grace invited me over to her parent's place for a weekend. While we were having fish and taro for tea, Grace's father asked me again about my motivation for my life. "I know I asked you already about your vision. I just want to know what your motivation is for waking up every morning, doing what you do."

I wanted to explain everything to him in detail.

"I was born and raised in a small village called Asi Asi in the north. My parents were subsistence farmers, working the land for their daily livelihood and survival. They both passed away due to illness. After their passing, I was left under the custody of my aunt. She is a widow with two kids. Her husband went fishing and never came home. He disappeared at sea. A search was conducted to no avail. She sent me to Fa'ato Primary School with her two kids to get an education. With the passage of time, we parted when I went to high school. I applied for a scholarship and was granted one to study Human Resource Management for three years at a prestigious college. Everything was paid for. At college, I met a fellow student with the same skin pigmentation as me. We became good friends and, in fact, were inseparable. We were like a couple, and I treated her as a friend.

"As the academic semester progressed, she developed feelings for me. I am a bit musical. I play the guitar, bass, and drums. She set me up to sing a song for her at the park where she overstepped her boundaries. I went from being a whole number to a fraction at the park. I thought I was in love.

"It was all smooth sailing until one rainy day, our secret affair was leaked. We were at the library, and it was raining heavily. A fellow student named Sarah Nanagalio learned of our affair first. We were standing behind the library, and I was holding this woman I loved, looking into her eyes as if she was legally mine. We thought no one was around.

As I was going to kiss her, Sarah saw us kissing and told her fellow countryman. This man was a fellow student, too, and loved the same girl I loved. He had adored her back home, but he hadn't taken initiative. He came out and threw a punch at my face. I acted in self-defense, and he landed on the ground like a dead man, unconscious and blood running from his forehead. It happened in about ten seconds. The police and the ambulance came. He was rushed to the hospital and ended up in a coma. The police whisked me away and put me in custody. I appeared in court and was found guilty of assault and inflicting bodily harm. I was slandered and libeled by a female witness. I served my time in jail, and was deported out of the country upon my release from jail."

Grace was listening and paying very close attention to my narrative.

"I landed at the airport and was picked up by a beautiful woman from Lord Howe islands. She teaches grammar at Oasis Grammar school. It was a coincidence. She didn't know why she had driven past the airport at that moment and time. She took me to her brother's place because the two sisters that had I lodged with before I left for college had moved to a new location."

"Is she married or single?" Grace asked.

"She was single, but why she is, I don't know. She is in her mid-forties now. She introduced herself as Miss Nofu Atkins. She suggested lodging with her brother until I was ready to go home. I agreed. I stayed with the Atkins family and told them my story. They were understanding and compassionate. They sent me home with a little bit of money to start a piggery because they knew that I had had experience doing this when I was in grammar school.

"I arrived home and rendered a public apology to the whole community. In a community, when it comes to success, it's a public interest, not personal. Success is not personal in a community. Everybody assembled in the house of meeting. I begged for forgiveness, and it was granted. They accepted me back into the community. After waiting for more than six months, my aunt started me off with two pigs: a male and a female. I used the money that the Atkins family gave me to buy mill run. The two pigs were fruitful and multiplied many times over, and today, I have five boys working with me full time.

"Now, as to the motivation behind this whole thing, it had to do with the tragic death of a mother and son because they were illiterate. I was in primary school when the incident happened. The son went with a few other boys to see a tourist boat berthing in the harbor. On their way home from seeing the boat, the son saw white bags piled beside the footpath in a cocoa plantation. He thought they were salt for seasoning because of the packaging—it was actually fertilizer—so he took a couple home and poured it into the salt container without his mother's knowledge. The mother was illiterate, too.

"The poor mother returned home from the garden, cooked soup, and poured the fertilizer into the soup. They ate the soup, and they were vomiting profusely and rushed to the hospital. They passed away from internal complications a few days later. There was no money to pay for transport to bring their bodies back home for proper burial. The truck that rushed them to the hospital was hired to transport people to a traditional wedding ceremony on the south side of the island and could not get back in time to bring the bodies home. The hospital's ambulance was broken down, too, and they were waiting for the part to arrive from Japan. As a result, the mother and son were buried in a cemetery close to the hospital, far away from home. Their loved ones and relatives did not have the chance to say goodbye to the mother and her son.

"I was utterly devastated. From that moment, I felt obligated to find solutions to the two problems that had given birth to this this tragedy: illiteracy and lack of money. Now I am solving the first problem of lack of money by making too much money and tucking it away in the bank. I have solved this problem by creating and making too much money through the piggery farm. Grace works at the bank and can testify to what I'm saying. Now that's paradoxical, but Grace can attest to my assertion."

"Listening to you talk is like watching a movie. I am intrigued and impressed by your story. So how do you intend to solve the second problem, the problem of illiteracy?" Mr. Masisimia asked.

"I want to build a school, a literacy training school, where students can attend for free. Student will learn for free, but there is an earning part to it as well. There will be a department in the school called "Read to Earn." This is how it works. You read and summarize a book and the school will check against their summarized copy, and if it matches, the school will pay you for the time you spent reading the book. The school pays a dollar a page. If you are reading and summarizing a two-hundred-page book, you get paid two hundred dollars; three hundred pages, three hundred dollars; and so forth. The school teaches you the skills and the mechanics of reading comprehension, then you apply the skills right in the school, reading books at the library. You don't need to go looking for a school to apply what you've learned. You learn and apply what you learned in the school.

"There is another department called the Destiny School of Finance. It teaches students how to manage and use the money they earn for maximum benefits. You know, money is a tool, like a drill or a chisel. You can hurt yourself if you don't know how to use it. It can be extremely helpful or extremely painful, depending on your knowledge of it. It can bring you joy and pain simultaneously. Those will be the two departments in the school for the students to equip themselves with the skills to manoeuvre in the real world. I will teach in the Destiny School of Finance, too, purely from my personal experience with money. I am very good with money, earning and managing it, and I would love to teach people what I've learned about money over the years.

"This school will be financially independent. It will generate its own money from businesses it establishes. It has its own business arm, and the business arms are economically sound and environmentally friendly. After being in the piggery business for about four years, I am convinced and can boldly say that money is not a problem. The problem is the lack of thinking and ideas. Initially, I thought money was the problem when the tragedy happened, but not anymore. I've realized and enjoyed the enormous and tangible benefits of having 'too much money.' Money is not a problem with the school. The school will have too much money like its board of directors," I said, laughing out loud.

"That's how I intend to solve the second problem. I will use the solution of the first problem, which is too much money, to fund the school with its Read to Earn program and the Destiny School of Finance, also known as DSOF," I said. "Furthermore, I will legislate a company policy for employment. We will recruit workers to work in our businesses only for five years. From entry to exit, a person will work for only a period of five years. There is no place for permanency within our businesses. There is no longevity of employment within our companies. This will give everybody a shot at this opportunity. This will enable and force people to organize and be more disciplined to keep track of every cent they spend and plan their finances to pursue their individual dreams and callings in life.

"As a company, we will train, equip, and empower them with information, and perhaps, inject resources to some extent if necessary. That is our obligation: to ensure that you are trained and equipped to start your own business, and the best time to do that is when you are vibrant and energetic. One shouldn't be forced to wait until you are exhausted from working for twenty to thirty years. There is no guarantee of long-term employment with us. There will be a time for every employee to leave. After five years, we expect people to pursue their dreams and visions in life."

"I love the short-term employment policy. If it is legislated and enacted, it will enable people to reform their bad spending habits and cultivate some good money habits. It will cause people to pause and determine the return on their investment for buying a certain product, and not succumb to impulse buying just to impress other people," said Mr. Masisimia.

"You're exactly right. I am living proof of what I am sharing with you. With the very little money that the Atkins family gave me, today, it has multiplied many times over in ways that I could not have even begun to imagine. When they gave me the money, they said it was their seed, and they entrusted that seed to me to plant it in the right environment to bring forth the expected harvest. With some basic management practices and discipline, I believe people can achieve and live their dreams in their lifetimes. Because if you can't manage the little that you have been entrusted with, you can't manage the big things. I am convinced that the most absent component in most people's lives is management, management of time and resources. People must develop and cultivate the discipline to retain their money and make it grow.

"Letting people work for me too long will breed complacency, and they won't launch out into what they are passionate about in the world. Not only am I living proof, but I've seen it worked in my boys' lives. The habit of saving that I taught them has literally transformed their lives in immeasurable ways. It didn't take long for them to realize the benefits of working and saving in a tangible manner. It is paying off big time. Most of them only have a second- or third-grade education. But they were hungry and wanted to do something worthwhile with their time," I concluded.

"I think I have heard enough, and I'm extremely satisfied for you to marry my daughter. I hope she knows by now the enormity of the task that lies ahead. At least she knows what she is getting herself into, the cost and the demand of a vision," her father said. "Alright, anything else you want to ask or say, sweetheart?"

"I am so happy that my beautiful daughter is going to marry a man who is going somewhere in life," his wife said. And I believe that Grace will do everything in her power to support you in your endeavours. One final thing I'm asking of you, my daughter, is to please make us proud and don't let us down in your conduct or in your speech."

"Okay everybody, let's call it a night. Let us know the date for the wedding," her father said. "It's a pleasure and honor to meet you. You are a visionary. I declare tonight, the seventh day of May, that Grace is now yours, and I release my blessing on her as a father. I am so thrilled that Grace has found another father, like me," he said.

Grace and I, together with Yagayo and Mercy, entered into courtship. We all learned more about each other during our courtship period, and we agreed to sleep and live with the things we saw in each other for the rest of our lives, until death. We all agreed to have our weddings on the same day. This wasn't much of a hurdle because we had all taken care of the financial burden that worries most people when it comes to marriage. Financial stability for Grace and Mercy had been taken care off by me and Yagayo long before we met these two beautiful women. All four of us were assets, and we would surely enrich, enhance, build and bring out the best in each other. What a powerful combination.

While we were enjoying our courtships, Mercy thought of a college girlfriend who was working as a registered nurse at the hospital. Her name was Ms. Esther Masasaolia. She was single and hardworking, saving money to build her mother a house.

"Hey, Grace, I was thinking about Esther Masasaolia who works at the hospital, Mercy said. "We are getting married soon to the ones we love, and we are inviting her to our weddings. She might feel left out, as her biological clock is ticking and the sun is setting behind the horizon. She told us she is saving money to build a house for her mom."

"You want to suggest something to her?" Grace asked.

"I'm thinking of seeing if one of Maduku's boys would be right for her," Mercy said. "I think we should catch up with her on Saturday, when she is not working, so we can talk over lunch or something."

"Sounds sweet," Grace said.

Mercy and Grace met up with Esther for lunch at the Ocean Breeze Hotel. They ordered something other than the usual fish and chips. They looked at the menu and ordered seafood for a change. While they were eating, Mercy mentioned the reason for meeting. "The reason we called you for lunch is that Grace and I are engaged to two boys from the village. They are pig farmers. We met them at the bank when they were our clients. We dropped those two we had been dating. She dropped Samson, and I dropped Ahimaaz."

"Congratulations to both of you. Now I'm the only single one left. I'm a hopeless romantic, just busy working and not socializing much," she said. "I've often wondered if maybe all the good men are taken already."

Esther sat down and continued. "I often think men feel shy to approach me for fear of rejection because of my profession or something. Or maybe they're scared of the sun's sign inscribed on my face, which clearly indicates which region I come from. But not all men charge and demand crazy dowry payments for their daughters. To say that every family is the same when it comes to dowry payments is a myth that I strongly refute. Every family is different. You get a better deal when you sit down and actually talk with the parents, and an understanding of one's situation might work in one's favor. Some people get the misconception that girls from my region cost as much as a streamliner or a new automobile or the cost of an airplane.

"My parents said they would not charge much for me. Whatever the lucky man can afford, he can give to satisfy the extended family members. At least they know he pays something because of our custom," she said.

"Don't worry, Esther. We've got you covered! We found a better way to find you a good man. We've been through the process ourselves, and so far so good," Grace said. "The results are fantastic, we're happier now more than ever."

"We both work at the bank, as you know, and there is this group of boys with their boss who deposit more money than we have seen in our entire lives. They live in the village and have never been to college, except for their boss but he didn't finish. Maduku is the boss and the founder of the piggery business where they work."

"They all single?" Esther was curious.

"They're all single, including their boss," Mercy said.

"So who's dating the founder?" Esther asked.

"Grace is," Mercy answered.

"Grace, you are a rich lady now, dating the founder of a business." They all laughed.

"These boys all have savings in the bank. They have too much money, and Mercy can attest to what I'm saying. The amount of money they have in their accounts is mind-blowing. They are just in their mid-twenties. Maduku, their leader, is nearing thirty. With the discipline and dedication that they have demonstrated, I can tell that these boys are going places. We have never stumbled across a group of boys like this, ever, never," Grace said.

"If it's okay with you, and you feel that you are ready, I will talk with Maduku to check with Isaiah, the third oldest in the group. You know, jump onboard and go for a cruise, and see if there is any compatibility," Mercy said.

"That's a good idea. I am starting to worry, too. Some of my work-mates are getting married already. When I saw them holding hands and walking down the hallway at the hospital, I wondered what was wrong with me. I often asked the question, 'Why is life so unfair? Why am I still single? I should just die in the tunnel. You know, as a girl, it's tough to see your friends settling down when you aren't," Esther said.

"I know, I know where you're coming from. We all been there, but we found a way out of it, at least for the two of us," Grace said. "I will talk with Maduku and see how it goes, okay?"

Grace caught up with me at the bank, and we had lunch together. While we were eating, Grace gingerly approached the question. "Hey

Maduku, I was wondering something."

"What are you wondering about?"

"About Isaiah?"

"Yes, what about him?"

"Is he seeing someone right now or not? Like, is he involved with someone? Mercy and I have a friend—we were together at college—she studied nursing and is now working at the hospital as a registered nurse. We thought of inviting her to our weddings, but were concerned she might feel left out because we are getting married and she's not. We had lunch with her on Saturday and found out she is not dating anyone. She expressed some disappointment, asking why life's so unfair, why no one approaches her. It's frustrating and emotionally straining for her just to think about it, especially when we told her that we are engaged. She is a good girl, hearty and compassionate. She deserves a good man to sweep her off her feet," Grace said.

"Which region does she come from?" I asked.

"She is from the North East," Grace answered.

"Does she have a star sign, like the rays of the sun, inscribed on her face?" I wanted to know.

"Yes she does," Grace answered.

"Now I know what scares most blokes from approaching her. The dowry payment for a girl from that region is unreal," I said.

"Yeah, but she said that's a myth, that every family is different. A common understanding to lower the dowry payment could be reached if both parties actually sit down and compromise," Grace said.

"Alright, I'll speak to Isaiah and hear what his thoughts are about this matter," I assured her.

I spoke with Isaiah about going on a date with Esther Masasaolia. This was an arrangement based on my good faith in the girls. They had known Esther since college and said she is a good girl. They had concerns for her happiness. That's what true friends and sisters do. They look out for each other because they have each other's interests at heart.

Isaiah agreed to a date. He had only finished second-grade, like Yagayo. The modest income his father could earn from cutting copra wasn't enough to pay for his school fees to finish formal schooling. Nevertheless, the money he was earning now on the piggery farm was more than most of his classmates who continued on to high school and probably ended up at college or university had in their bank accounts. He was happy working on the farm. Even though he didn't have a college diploma or degree, he never complained.

He reached the conclusion that whether you have a college diploma or not, the value of money that one earns is the same. The same hundred-dollar bill that the guy working in the office earns, the guy working on the piggery farm earns, too. The value of a dollar is the same. The only thing that warmed his heart was that he was amassing too much money. Making too much money was a joyful thing for Isaiah. It was the culture on the piggery farm, the common bond they all shared. They never talked about money on the farm. They only talked about ideas. Having too much money was a natural expression of the disciplines they had cultivated and applied. Grace, Mercy and I arranged for Isaiah and Esther to meet, to get to know each other, and to see if there was chemistry and compatibility between them.

Isaiah met Esther, and they clicked. They got engaged and went into courtship. Esther was right. Her family did not expect much from the lucky guy who was going to marry her, but Esther was happy that she had finally found love. Isaiah was well coached under my leadership in discipline and character, the qualities that all the boys had developed while working on the farm. Discipline was the force behind everything we did on the farm.

All three girls, all college graduates, had finally found someone to marry until death. Isaiah and Esther decided to walk down the aisle a year after Grace's and Mercy's wedding.

Meanwhile, Yagayo and I started building houses for our future wives. We built houses with three bedrooms. It took us two short months to build because we had the money to do it quickly. While our houses were being built, we booked the Saturday, the second week of November, for our weddings. My community knew about the wedding, including my family and relatives. I also wrote to inform the Atkins family of the wedding date with the hope that they would be able to come.

# Chapter 17

# Maduku Solves Problems

The second Saturday in the month of November arrived. The Atkins family and Grace and Mercy's coworkers from the bank descended on Asi Asi village. The parents of the brides and the relatives of the grooms were excited to see their kids finally enter the most important institution on the planet, marriage.

The community and the chief were excited to see that I, their son Maduku, had bounced back from failure and emerged stronger for my struggles. And now I was about to take the most sacred oath made between life and death. The priest who was going to officiate the two weddings had just recently graduated from seminary with a diploma in theological studies.

Our vows were spoken amidst a great cloud of witnesses, the rings exchanged and placed on the fingers of the brides and the grooms. The priest proclaimed the couples to be husbands and wives in the presence of the people. It was a moving and touching moment, a memorable one for everybody in the congregation. Maduku's boys, as they had come to be known, were excited to see their boss finally settled down, and Yagayo, the one who had introduced them to me in their pursuit for change, was also entering into that sacred institution. The groomsmen were the four boys, and the bridesmaids were work colleagues of Grace and Mercy. All of them were still single. This occasion presented a perfect opportunity for the single women working at the bank to see men with vision and discipline instead of only people with diplomas and degrees who were going nowhere in life with their academic qualifications.

Those from the bank were excited and knew that Grace and Mercy had made the right choice in marrying me and Yagayo, in spite of our lack of educational background. They knew very well that we would meet and address every one of our brides' crucial needs. That came from our financial stability. They knew that now Grace and Mercy would not have to work, but instead would choose to work. They were unsure and a bit nervous that Grace and Mercy might stop working and leave the bank to work for another financial institution, especially the General Manager who was a woman with a master's degree in business and finance. She harbored doubts about Grace and Mercy's future with the bank. She knew that Yagayo and the boys and I had plenty of money in the bank, and the bank makes more money through lending. Any move orchestrated by Grace and Mercy would have a drastic impact on the bank's financial aspirations. She reckoned it was best to talk with them directly to find out their thoughts.

After the official part of the ceremony was over, then came the food, everyone's favorite part. Yagayo and I had killed twelve pigs for our weddings. There was food in abundance, organic and locally grown in the gardens of the people.

While everybody was having a good time eating and enjoying their food, I got up and made a short speech, thanking all of those amazing people who had been with me every step of the way since I had been expelled from college. "First, I would like to thank my parents who are no longer here with us, but I know they are watching. I know my debt to them is beyond measure. I am grateful for the discipline and hard work they instilled in me. To my aunt, who took on that awesome responsibility after my parents passing, thank you for all the sacrifices you have made. I am forever grateful. To the Atkins family who is here with us today. Thank you for believing in me. You showed up in the darkest hours of my life when it seemed like all the stars in my sky had fallen. Especially Ms. Nofu, who I believe was an angel in disguise. Thank you for the hope and destiny you have given me. It was not by accident, but a divine coincidence in my opinion, and the rest is history.

"Thank you for showing me what it means to be men and women of principle. To Mrs. Atkins, you are the epitome and the embodiment of womanhood. You showed me what a woman should be in private and in public. You exhibited that in the way you dress and in your speech. I have learned so much from you, my dear Atkins family. I would also like to thank my amazing community, the chief, and the people of Asi Asi village. Thank for accepting my apology, and welcoming me back into the community. I would not be where I am today without the unyielding support you have shown and given me since the birth of the piggery farm.

"To my amazing team, who have pioneered with me every step of the way to this very day, I am so proud of you. You have made me proud through your commitment to service and duty, duty to yourself and to one another. We are where we are today because of you. We play as a team and we win as a team. We will continue to win if we maintain that spirit of teamwork, standing and sticking up for each other. I believe we will continue to work as a team to do more good in the years ahead.

"Last but not the least, I would like to thank the girl who agreed to marry me today, Ms. Grace Mamata. She used to be Ms. Masisimia, but she just converted to Mamata a few hours ago at the altar. She looked past my flaws, my mistakes, and my educational background. I want you to know that you are the most wonderful and beautiful thing that ever happened to me. Despite all that you have heard and seen and my initial reluctance to say yes to your proposal, I am in awe of your persistence and unwavering faith to make this day a reality. Marriage is like a rose flower. There are thorns on the rose, too. And I am committed to love the rose with its thorns as long as I live, and that is you. I will endeavour to make your happiness my priority above all else that I do. I need your help and support to make me a better father, husband, and most important, your best friend. I want you to know that you are my precious jewel that I have found. Welcome to my adventure. Thank you very much, everybody." I looked around at all who had my life possible, thanking them again with a nod of my head.

Ms. Nofu, representing the Atkins family, also shared a few remarks about her encounter with me. She was so thrilled that I was now part of the Atkins family, and she was also amazed that she had learned the traditional way of food preservation in a bamboo where there is no refrigeration and power. She told how she had learned that the bamboo has multiple uses. You can use it to store drinking water, use it as a torch at night, weave leaves for thatch houses, and use it as rafters for a house or as a knife for cutting meat. It's also a reservoir of water in the jungle if you are thirsty. It is a life-saving tree, an amazing tree, the bamboo tree. Nofu also said they would love to keep in touch with my family and would love to visit again to witness the birth of any great plan that I would put into action. She was blown away by the amazing work that the boys and I had done. The piggery business was mind-blowing. To achieve that level of success in a few years was unimaginable, but she was not really surprised because she understood the power of principles. The bank manager also offered a few remarks on behalf of her staff. She was excited for Grace and Mercy, and hoped they would stay and work for the bank until they had babies, even if they had much money in the bank due to their husbands' success. She congratulated them and wished them long life and happiness in marriage, in business, and in life.

Joseph Yagayo, too, spoke of his early encounter with me, which had brought tremendous change to his life. Without me, he said, he would not be where he was. He had found change without a preacher or someone visiting and knocking on his door with a religious brochure or pamphlet. He had found change through the manifestation of "words becoming deeds," just as in my life. He was attracted and drawn to my lifestyle because it was like a tree with fruits. For him, it had been a private encounter and experience, the day that he found me. Neither his mother nor his friends knew about it. He regarded our encounter as a meeting with destiny. And from that day on, all of his friends had followed and found change, meaning, and purpose for their lives.

Grace and Mercy both stayed with the bank for another two years even after being married. Grace tendered her resignation in the third year because I suggested that it was time for her to work full time with me to achieve the vision in my heart. Mercy tendered her resignation the same year Grace did. The bank was so sad to see them leave because they had been committed and dedicated workers. A farewell party was held and the staff wished them all the best in their future endeavours. Working for money was no longer a necessity for Grace and Mercy. They could now work for joy with their husbands in the piggery business. They handled the accounting and administration side of the business. They would still do business with the bank, even though they no longer worked for the bank. They would call in to have a chat with their former workmates when they deposited money at the bank.

As time went on, I felt that I needed the expertise of a qualified person to assist with the business, to ensure quality meat for the butchers. Manning an operation of two thousand and five hundred pigs was a hefty task, so I spoke with my team about engaging the expertise of an agriculturalist who worked for a big abattoir which had shut down after an ethnic crisis that had crippled the economy.

The expert joined my team. He helped secure a tractor for farming cassava and pumpkins to supplement the mill run. He helped install a water pump for drinking and cleaning the piggery house. We noticed that sales increased dramatically. That was the beauty of engaging an expert.

The pumpkin and cassava farm was planted and harvested. There were so many pumpkins and cassava, that the people at Bubulu village came and filled their baskets to feed their families.

As the operation grew to the next level, the expert and I started getting engagements to speak at villages in the district about the success of the piggery business. People wanted to hear the story behind our success. People had seen the impact of the piggery business in the lives of the boys from Bubulu village. For many years, they had been feeding pigs as a hobby. But when I arrived, I revolutionized and commercialized the entire product and industry, taking it to a whole new level. The youth were inspired, and the model was duplicated in other villages with our help and assistance. It was phenomenal and revolutionary.

# Chapter 18

## Without Vision, People Perish

As the success of the piggery business reached unprecedented heights, I felt it was time to deal with the second problem, the problem of illiteracy. I discussed this with the team. The second part of my vision was to create a literacy training center for young and old to attend for free. It didn't matter what age the students were. I had already mentioned this second phase to my father in-law, and Grace knew about it and was inspired.

"For those of you who don't know, there are actually two problems that I feel compelled and obligated to solve in life. They are the motivation for my existence. They are the reason why I get up every morning doing what I am doing now. I was in primary school when a tragedy happened. A mother and son died of food poisoning because they were illiterate.

"The son mistook fertilizer for salt, for food seasoning. They were rushed to the hospital and died a few days later. The hospital's ambulance was broken down, and the only transport in our area at that time was hired for a wedding in the eastern part of the island. As a result, they were buried at a cemetery close to the hospital. Their loved ones and family members didn't have the chance to say goodbye. So their tragic death gave birth to two problems, as far as I was concerned: the problem of illiteracy and the problem of lack of money. Those are the two problems that motivated and compelled me to find solutions. The first problem, as you all aware, we have solved. We have been making much money through sales. We have enough money to enable us to do anything we put our minds to.

"I feel like we solved the problem with enough money, and that makes me glad. When the tragedy happened, I was devastated, but now I'm happy. This is what I struggle to understand: If something is already available and is flowing like a current, and I mean money, why not make more of it when you can? It doesn't hurt to make more. Actually, making more of it is good, so we can put it in as many hands as possible, but not just any hands. You can put money in the hand of those with a vision and a plan of execution for that vision. So I want to put as many tools as possible in the hands of those with a plan to get important work done.

"Additionally, manufacturing as many tools as we possibly can make life worth living for me. It's fun and joyful to watch and get involved. That's the assignment I was given. I love making money and making large amounts is fun and exciting. In fact, having too much of it is not evil. It is *how* one uses it that determines whether it's evil or not. It's like having a hammer, chisel, circular saw, or drill. You use it to get work done. After you use it, you tuck it away in a cupboard for future use. Or if someone wants to borrow it to get work done, you lend it to them.

"When others finish using your tools (money), they give it back to you to keep and lend to the next person who needs it to get important work done. And when that person finishes, they give it back to you, again, for others. You keep it for lending and distribution. I call that wise management. That's my philosophy about money. It is a tool, a conduit. When spent wisely, invested wisely, It is a means to constant improvement and growth. It's when we try to hoard money that we get into serious problems. Hence, I want us to continue to carry forward what we are doing to the next level.

"So this is how we are going to implement the second phase of the vision as a team. We will build a school, and I have already talked with my beautiful wife about the name for the school. I want to call the school Destiny Literacy Training Centre or DLTC. There will be no fees charged to enroll. Everybody is welcome to learn how to read and write. But there is an earning part to the program. I would like to call that part the "Read to Earn" department. We will build a library for the school and hire literature professionals to write written book reports about the books, their content, and message. We will have the summarised report and copy of the book in the reserve section.

When a student reads a book and submits a written book report about the book he or she reads, the staff will check the student's written book report to see if it matches the copy in the reserve section. If it does match, the school will pay one dollar for each page read. The student earns according to the number of pages in that book he or she summarises. One hundred pages, one hundred dollars, two hundred pages, two hundred dollars, and so forth. The school will teach them all the mechanics and skills of reading comprehension, and the types of reading methods that exist in the literature world.

"You will apply what you learned in the school and earn money while learning. What do you all think?" I asked the team.

"That's a brilliant idea. I love it," said the agriculturalist. "I know a couple. They are both teachers. They've been teaching English in different countries for more than thirty years. I can talk to them if you don't have anyone particular in mind. They both graduated with master's degrees in English and literature."

"That's awesome. I don't have anyone in mind, really. Please talk to them, and we'll set up a time to meet and talk about how best we can employ their expertise, and we will give them contracts to sign if we are satisfied with what we hear," I said, continuing to spell out my vision to my team.

"The second phase of the vision is pretty much like running the piggery operation. You can make a living by learning to read and write book reports. The piggery operation and other income-generating ventures will fuel money to keep them running. Also, the school will have its own business arms to support its administration and staff in terms of wages and salaries and supplies. I also have a few business ideas that I want to toss on the table. I want us to establish businesses that are economically sound and friendly to the environment, that are not destructive. I would like us to start with beekeeping, then move on to others. I'll check with a bee specialist who used to work for the government to see if he is available to start us off. We need ten beehives, and then we can expand from there. What do you folks think about beekeeping?"

"I love bees for their tremendous contribution to the planet with respect to pollination," Isaiah said.

"And once we are up and running strong, we can venture into other businesses. Another business I've identified is an aquarium in nature. There is huge potential in the aquarium sector. I want us to name our company "Next Level Companies." Everything we do, including the school and the companies, we will do it with class and excellence. I also want us to put into legislation a five-year employment policy. We will employ people for five years, and after five years, we expect them to leave and pursue their passion and calling in life. We will train, equip, and empower them with the mental tools and skills they might need. We will help them with financial resources if necessary to start them off. We want them to know that there is no permanency with our companies.

"Giving people an exit time frame is good for many reasons. First, it will help people to cultivate the habit of saving money. Second, it enables and forces people to reform their bad spending habits on unnecessary things that didn't contribute to their vision. It reduces impulse buying. Third, it helps people to prioritize and organize their finances. It wakes people up from laziness and procrastination. We want people to know that we are only here on this earth for so long. We don't have forever to do what we were born to do. We only have a certain number of seasons in life to execute the dreams and visions in our hearts.

"Giving people an indefinite time to work for us will breed complacency and stagnancy. People will become static and not creative because it is routine and mundane. The environment is not vibrant anymore because there is no variety. Permanency might increase production but stifle creativity on the part of the workers. Mastery of a skill is good for increased production, but it suffocates drive and energy necessary for entrepreneurship.

When people are hungry, vibrant, and energetic, release them into their calling before boredom kicks in. There is nothing wrong with permanency, but I don't want to trap people for the rest of their lives so that they aren't able to give birth to the amazing ideas in their heads, that dream or vision that they have. We don't want to hold people hostage working for us, and keep them from pursuing and manifesting their trees with its fruit to bless humanity and the world. Our companies are just stepping stones or launching pads. We want our companies to be the training ground for people to pursue their callings in life.

"I know it's not my business to dictate how people should live their lives, but I want our companies to be different. I don't want our companies to be treated as a place to earn money and squander it. This is the wrong place and environment for that kind of mindset and attitude. We want people who work for us to be different in how they manage the resources life has given to them," I continued. "We want to see their written plan and life's vision when they apply to work for us. They must provide a written plan and vision prior to applying for a job with any of our companies."

I was indeed a visionary. My team embraced my philosophy and believed that everything I said was possible and achievable if they continued to improve on the discipline and work ethic they applied in the piggery business and in their personal finances. They had seen a glimpse and tasted a portion of my vision already, and they were hungry for more because they had found joy and fulfillment working for change in the district. What they had achieved gave them hope for what they could and must achieve tomorrow.

The agriculturalist spoke with his friends about teaching conversational English at DLTC. They agreed to join us, and they were impressed with my vision. I explained to them my vision for the school. I showed them the plan, and they loved it. They wanted to be part of what we were doing. They were shocked to see the piggery operation, the financial lifeblood of the school, and my team that was comprised of village boys who had never gone to college or university. They were satisfied with what they saw, and they signed the contractual paper agreements.

The team and I built a semi-permanent classroom to start the training center. We built one semi-permanent staff house for the couple to live in. It had a shower and toilet inside. The staff house and the classroom were solar-powered. Finally, the facilities were finished and ready for occupation. The couple moved into their new home. The classroom was also fitted with solar power and a bathroom and shower. The couple ate local food like taro, cassava, and banana, supplied by the community. Taking up the teaching job with the school, they knew that they could save more than three-quarters of their salary because there was no rent or bills to pay. They received a fresh supply of snapper and tuna fish on Saturdays without spending a dime. The school and the community looked after them, and they thought about telling their friends who were teaching abroad to come and teach with them when the school expanded. They wished they had taught in a school like mine forty years ago. Nonetheless, they were happy and worked to give the best that they could to the students. They tasted the generosity of the school and the community prior to the grand opening of the school, and there was nothing like it.

People came from the forgotten corners of the island to witness the opening of Destiny Literacy Training Centre, the first of its kind on the island, a place where one could learn and earn. People from different backgrounds and cultures converged on Asi Asi village, where the training center was built and situated. Most of the people came through word of mouth to witness this remarkable day, an event that would serve as a monument to success and revolution to both the born and unborn generations on the island.

During the grand opening, the first intake of students was announced. The class had twelve students: a couple in their mid-fifties, five boys from my team, two single mothers, and three women who were widows. The students were encouraged to speak their mother tongue and English. But at school, they are not allowed to speak or communicate in their mother tongue. They could do that at home. At school, English was the only language, and it was compulsory. Maintaining their mother tongue was their identity, and learning English was vital because the world was now interconnected, a global village.

The Honourable Minister for Education was the guest of honour for the opening. He applauded me and my pioneers for being the agents of change in the social and industrial development on the island. "It is an honor and a privilege to be part of this historic moment on our island. I am fortunate to be alive to see this day. Many people have said that this day would never come. Is anyone out there who still doubts, who still questions, and who still feels that you cannot live your dreams before you die? Today is your answer.

"It is possible to see and live your dreams during your lifetime if you are willing to do the work and the discipline that is required. It is my hope that you will go back to your homes with a new mindset from this day on, inspired and energized that anything is possible if you believe," said the education minister.

My team and I fed the people who had come for the opening, so they would have the strength and energy to travel back to their respective homes and villages.

I made my intentions clear to the people, that I wanted to expand opportunity and model for learning, job creation and business development across the island. I asked for their cooperation in the opening and freeing up land for development. Some landowners had seen with their own eyes the good work done by my team, and they had already decided to free up land, so the same opportunity could be offered and available to their people. They had been waiting for such a model for a while, and now they had seen and witnessed the model being implemented by one of their very own on the island and with their very own eyes. They confessed that their reservation and reluctance to free up land was because there had always been too much talk and too little action before. And most of the activities carried out in other tribal lands in the name of development was destructive to the environment. They were mainly logging activities. Now they had seen something that was environmentally friendly to nature and offered equal opportunity to every willing heart who wanted to take a shot in life regardless of their personal background or upbringing.

Soon, the beekeeping project was up and running, generating more money through honey extraction.

My team and I ventured into the farming of eels, prawns, and mud crab. I was active in finding markets for these products overseas. I was instrumental in sourcing buyers for the eels, prawns, and crabs that we were farming. The people who worked for me were surprised to see how much money was just tucked away in plain sight, in the things that people had overlooked for years and decades. For too long, the people had set their sights on things that weren't tangible, the gimmick of getting rich overnight and becoming an instant millionaire. The resources I discovered were not new. They had just been ignored and overlooked.

The beauty of these resources, in contrast to resources of a different nature, was that you controlled what you sold, you knew how much you packed in a box and sent to the market. That was the beauty of the aquarium resources.

My boys attended classes in the morning till twelve, and their conversational English had improved dramatically. They were bold and confident when talking with tourists in the little town. I told them to be sure to journal. I encouraged them to buy cameras and take photos and store them in an album. I told them about the importance of journaling and taking photos. "Jotting down your thoughts in a journal and taking photos serves one important purpose: they are the treasures that you will leave behind for your kids, grandkids and future generations to enjoy."

They might not talk about a car or a house when they arrive—there is no emotion in them—but journals and photos will give them something to talk about during Christmas or at a family reunion. They can recognize the people in the photos and the good times they shared when they were alive. The photos serve as a reservoir of fond memories to cherish and to lean on for comfort and inspiration when life is unkind and unfair. Their thoughts in a journal might inspire them to keep pursuing their dreams and never give up. I am doing the same. I jot down my thoughts and events that happen in my life every day.

The boys bought cameras and albums and started taking photos. They had found a new hobby, and they loved it. The knowledge of leaving behind their thoughts and emotions in a book for the enjoyment of family, relatives and friends after they had died made it more rewarding, fulfilling, and encouraging to keep writing at the end of each day. When the students from Bubulu village saw the boys' journals, they, too, were inspired and started journaling.

After the opening of Destiny Literacy Training Centre, my team and I got back to work. My boys attended class, then worked in the piggery business from noon until 6:00 in the evening. They had Saturdays and Sundays off for family and recreation activities. They also established the aquarium businesses and employed people from villages in the district.

Not long after the opening of the training centre, Grace became pregnant with twin boys. Two years later, she was pregnant again with twins, and this time, they were girls. I was so excited. My love for my wife has never changed. Instead, with the passage of time, it grows more each day, as the years go by.

The literacy school is doing well. One of the students from Bubulu village named Ishmael Raomalefo actually wrote a book report and earns his first two hundred dollars. He was excited and couldn't believe that he had earned money for just reading and writing a book report. His mother encouraged him to continue reading and writing book reports because he was lazy at gardening, fetching water, and gathering firewood for cooking and lighting. He was good at note-taking from written texts and lectures. He continued to read and continued to earn and build his mother her first home. Now, he never leaves the library. He reads and his word wealth is huge, enabling him to confidently speak without having to look at notes when he was asked to present a speech in his village during church commemoration ceremonies.

Everybody was convinced that the "Read to Earn" curriculum was actually working. Ishmael is living testament that it does works! More people could not wait to enroll at Destiny Literacy Training Centre, even students who were already learning the mainstream curriculum but could not read properly. Their parents withdrew them and put them in DLTC. The results at DLTC are impressive and exceptional, and earning while learning is the beauty of Destiny Literacy Training Centre. It's the icing on the cake.

Maduku was now a husband, father, mentor, businessman, and best friend to his wife. He eventually solved the two problems he had been faced with. Literacy training was now available and free. Lack of money had now become too much money if you were willing to work, and there was work available. Urban drift for young people was under reversed as jobs were now available near home. Most young people who were living with relatives in the city and not working were returning home to make something out of their lives. There was work in abundance, and literacy training spread across the island. People freed up land for development because they saw the benefits and tangible results of what I was doing, transforming lives for the better.

After Isaiah and Esther's wedding, Isaiah told me that he wanted to explore the possibility of converting swine manure into gold. I gave him the freedom to pursue that idea and make it a reality. Branching out from the organization was a sign of maturity, and I assured Isaiah that if he needed help, my doors are always open.

Epilogue

Two years later, Samson Galorodo and Ahimaaz Soekeni graduated from university and returned home. They managed to graduate, even though their marks weren't good. They got C's in their final assessments, blaming heir unsatisfactory performance on grace and mercy. This was because they were upset after being dumped by two girls named Grace and Mercy, for Maduku Mamata and Joseph Yagayo. They were expecting at least B's or B+ in their assessments. Getting C's was not good enough in their opinion. It was a bit unfortunate for them, but who were they to dictate how these two young women, Grace and Mercy, should live their lives and whom they should marry.

Upon returning home, Ahimaaz Soekeni heard from friends and relatives that Mercy had married someone in the village and had stopped working at the bank. Ahimaaz was heartbroken and decided to find a girl on another island, so he could marry and move permanently with her, to avoid seeing Mercy and her husband holding hands walking around town. He found one girl and moved away, never to return even when his mother passed away from old age.

Samson Galorodo, on the other hand, couldn't handle the heartbreak and the pain. When he heard that Grace had also married and stopped working at the bank, he committed suicide by drinking thirty capsules of chloroquine. They rushed him to the hospital, but he was pronounced dead upon arrival. Esther was at the hospital when Samson was pushed through on the stretcher into the emergency room, but it was too late. He was gone. His family sent out condolence messages on the national broadcasting service radio to relatives and friends, and schoolmates in and around the country who had known Samson as a friend, schoolmate, or close relation. It was tragic for someone well-educated like Samson to terminate his life in such a manner. He chose a permanent solution to a temporary problem. Grace and I also heard on our transistor radio the message that Samson Galorodo had died of a drug overdose on his way to the hospital. May his soul rest in peace. I am convinced and still believe that without vision, people perish.

www.ingramcontent.com/pod-product-compliance
Lightning Source LLC
Chambersburg PA
CBHW070949190726
48292CB00004B/1389